ILLUSION

S. EVEREST

Illusion

By S. Everest

playlist

Higher
EMBRZ

Sink or Swim
Pierce Fulton, Bebe Rexha

What do you want from me?
Bad Omens

I'll See You When the Night Comes
breakk.away

Antimatter
Silent Planet

Bitches Brew
††† (Crosses)

CONTORTIONIST
Arankai

Don't Give up on Me
ILLENIUM, Kill The Noise, Mako

The Diary of Jane – Single Version
Breaking Benjamin

The Apparition
Sleep Token

Falls (Reprise) – Instrumental
ODESZA

This book has an open-ended ending.
Some may consider it a cliffhanger.

This book contains sensitive subjects such as violence, gore, child abuse, drinking, drugs, adult language, and sexually explicit scenes.
It is *only* for those ages 18+.

There are also scenes with on-page rape and sexual assault.
Please proceed with caution.

1

The sharp silver sword slid in front of me, barely catching on my cream-colored bodysuit. With my palm, I gently pushed it away from my torso, giving me an extra centimeter of breathing room. The tip of the blade found its way out of the open space on the other side of the box. I blinked a few times, trying my best to acclimate to the darkness.

Another sword came in, this time from my left, and traveled straight across the front of my chest. Fuck, this was cutting it close. If I even *tried* to take in a deep breath, the sword would easily slice my skin open.

Holding my breath, I pressed my back against the wall of the box as hard as I could. A few seconds floated by as I waited for another sword, and sure enough, I heard the wood creak above me. Glancing up, I watched as the silver dagger descended through the top of the box. I kept my position still as the blade nestled in the space in front of me, only an inch away from the tip of my nose.

This wasn't one of my favorite magic tricks, but it was definitely one of the most popular. Here, we called it the "Box of Swords," and it always got a rise out of the audience. Bram, the magician, would put me in a tall, slender, wooden box. I would find my position, which was as far back as I could go, and watch for the swords to come through. Thankfully, we've done and practiced this enough for me to know the pattern. He starts on my right every time, then alternates sides until six blades are staggered across my body. Then, he finishes off with a sword from above, and I manage to guide it through the maze of steel in front of me so it doesn't get jammed or stuck.

Then, when the audience is full of anticipation, he pulls them all out one by one in the same order he put them in. There's no blood on any of them, which could be a good or bad sign, depending on whatever fate the audience wants for me.

Some people like blood.

Some people want gore.

Some people wish to see a twist of excitement.

Sadly, for those people, I come out of the box alive, unharmed, and sometimes with a small rip in my clothes.

With the silver blades gone and new room to breathe, I plastered a bright, fake smile on my face as Bram opened the door. Spotlights shined in my eyes, forcing my pupils to dilate as Bram extended his hand to me. I took it, stepped out of the box, and struck a pose to the one person sitting in the audience.

"Good," was all he said, his face undistinguishable from the combination of the lights flashing in my vision and the lack of brightness cast over the audience's section.

But then he stood, walked out of his row, and made his way toward the stage. That's when I could see him again.

Vark was a big, hefty man who could sweat for days, even in the coldest of temperatures. His thin combover was covered by a beige hat, and he wore the standard carnival attire: khaki pants, a white button-up shirt, and red suspenders that constantly fell to the sides due to his protruding stomach. Even though his appearance wasn't the most pleasing, he always had his head on straight while dealing with the business of the carnival.

He didn't fuck around when it came to acts here. Everyone had to be top-notch, and if you weren't, you were gone.

A cigar puffed from between his lips, the cherry red glow barely adding warmth to his greasy, sweaty skin.

"Can you do it all again in a few weeks?"

"Of course," Bram answered, dropping my hand as if it was on fire. "In our sleep."

I managed to subtly roll my eyes, but luckily, it just came off as me casually scanning the room.

Vark nodded to us both in acceptance. At least he was pleased with us, which is more than some acts here could say.

As he turned to go, he took the cigar out from his lips and pointed to me. "Willa, find a different outfit. That rip tells people how the trick is done."

I looked down at my cream-colored bodysuit, and in the light, I could see a small snag near my right hip.

Fuck. This was one of my good stage outfits.

As Vark left the room, I watched his slow stride as the smoke from his cigar followed him out. Since the moment I stepped foot on this island, there have been rumors floating around that Vark isn't his real name. People say he got the name from simply running the ship, or "the leader of the arc," which conveniently shortened to Vark.

I like to think that he just looks like an aardvark.

After the tent closed behind Vark, I quickly trotted over to side stage as stagehands began disassembling our setup. I could hear and feel Bram follow me, and soon enough, I could feel his hand snake around the front of my hip. I reached for my grey sweatpants and unfolded them.

He buried his nose in the crook of my neck, and it took everything in me not to recoil. "Is this fixable?" he whispered against my skin, running his fingertips along the rip in my bodysuit.

"Probably not," I answered flatly, stepping into my sweatpants and pulling them up.

"Good," he said, and I could feel his grin on my shoulder. "Then I can rip it all the way off."

I forced myself to swallow my annoyance. "I'd rather not, Bram."

"Come on," he insisted, giving my hip a squeeze. "We always have fun."

Do we?

I turned to face him, and his hand remained on my hip. His dark hair fell neatly to the tops of his shoulders, his button-up shirt was hanging open, and his slacks were doing nothing to hide his growing erection. His eyes scanned me from the top of my strapped, neutral-colored shapewear to where it met my sweatpants, and I felt violated by his mental assessment. I tossed my red, curly hair over my shoulder and crossed my arms over my chest, doing what I could to shield myself from his eyes.

I opened my mouth to speak, but Bram cut me off before I could say anything.

"Alright, Willa. You want to do this here, right now, in front of everyone? Or do you want to do this the *easy* way?"

His hand reached for my elbow, but I jerked it away.

He let out a dry laugh. "Oh, so that's your choice?"

Before I could make another move, Bram grabbed me by both biceps, picked me up, and walked me toward the corner of the tent.

"Get *off* me, Bram."

All he did was let out a stupid chuckle.

While dodging my kicks and containing my squirms, he carried me to a spot behind stacked metal storage boxes. It wasn't enough to hide us completely, but it was enough for people to block us out and ignore us.

Which is what they always did.

Everyone here, workers and performers and everyone in between, thought we were a couple. We perform well together, we spend over ninety percent of our time together, and we know how to paint a pretty picture together.

But that's what we do best. *Magic.*

And as we all know, it's not real. None of it.

Bram threw me down onto the hard, dirty ground, causing the strap of my bodysuit to snap off one end.

"Aw, look. I don't even have to do the ripping. You're doing it for me."

Bram kneeled down in front of me and undid the button of his pants. I continued to kick him, but once his pants were down to his knees, he grabbed my bare feet and dragged me closer, fitting himself between my legs.

"Come on, my little magic rabbit. Don't fight me."

God, I fucking hated when he called me that.

Reaching up, I threw my arms at him, swinging at anything I could make contact with. His chest, his throat, even his perfect money-maker face. He blocked me from every angle and still managed to hold down my legs as well.

I began to run out of breath as he grabbed my sweatpants and yanked them down to my knees.

"Let's see if you're wet for me, baby," he whispered while hovering above me.

And that's when I gave up the fight.

Time and time again, Bram chased the high he got from performing and used me as a release.

Well, used *my pussy* as a release.

I don't think he really cared about *me*.

My fights were always futile, and my efforts never lasted. He was stronger, faster, and more powerful than me.

He was *always* more powerful.

With a quick snap of my body suit, the fabric coiled up toward my stomach, instantly giving him the access he wanted.

And with his dick free and ready, he quickly thrust inside me, not checking to see if I was actually wet or not.

I wasn't.

A slight, burning sting set fire to the space between my legs. It definitely wasn't comfortable, but it wasn't completely unbearable, either. Bram continued to rock his hips against me, the friction of our dry skin slowly becoming involuntarily wet with each movement. I tried to focus on his lips, his clean-shaven jaw, anything to feel a morsel of pleasure in this moment. It was my survival instinct kicking in.

And as obnoxious as it may be, Bram is good-looking. It's a fact.

His toned chest glistened under the faded tent lights. His arms could lift me with ease. His smile could light up a room.

And if he wasn't such a fucking asshole who liked to take advantage of me, he might be someone worth my time.

The first time he wanted to chase his high with me, I was more than willing. He was friendly, sweet, and full of genuine charisma, and I loved the attention he gave me. The sex was good—great, even—but soon after, I realized his interest in me was only surface-level. He didn't care about who I was or where I came from; he only cared about the way I made his dick pulse.

And when I tell him no, which I do at least once every time he tries to take me, he makes it known that I can lose my job here. All he has to do is cry out some pretty boy tears in a single conversation with Vark, and I'd be thrown out of the carnival.

After all, the magician's assistant is the most easily replaceable job here. All Bram needs is a beautiful girl who knows how to direct some swords.

So, after a brief and useless battle, I close my mouth and let him use my body.

Because if I can't be here, I have nowhere else to be.

The slamming sound of Bram's hips against mine was the only noise between us. He grabbed a fistful of my bodysuit and pulled it down, exposing my breasts. More ripping of the fabric sounded as he let out a shuddered moan. I laid still, in the dirt, while he released everything he had inside of me. His chest was heaving due to his lack of breath, and I could feel the warm liquid run down the skin of my ass the second he pulled out of me.

I hated that feeling.

I hated *all* of these feelings.

"You're still on the pill, right?" he asked, straightening up and fixing his pants.

You would think he would ask that *before* coming inside me.

He looked up and over the boxes to see if anyone was around, completely ignoring me and the lack of an answer I gave.

Before standing to his feet, he pressed his palm to my bent knee, giving it a slight jostle.

"Thanks, Willa."

Then, he left.

He left me in the dirt, lying behind boxes in the corner of the red-striped tent.

He left me by myself to fix my clothes, my hair, and to brush the dirt off my skin.

What once was a hand that helped me out of the "Box of Swords" was now a hand that didn't bother to help me up and out of the dirt.

I covered my face with my palms and sighed.

2

With a ripped bodysuit, dirt-scuffed pants, and the reminder of Bram oozing down my legs, I somehow managed to get up and find my way out of the tent; everyone's stares be damned. I grabbed the grey zip-up sweatshirt that matched my pants, put it on, and zipped it up as far as it could go while untucking my red hair from beneath the hood.

With a new embarrassment flushed on my cheeks and bile rising in my throat, I exited the tent and was immediately thrust into the hustle of everyone preparing for the upcoming week.

As if no one knew—or cared—that I just got raped twenty feet away from them.

Then again, why should they? I didn't scream. I only fought back for a minute before giving in.

How could I be the victim when I didn't do the most to stop it?

As I began walking, I quieted the voice in my head and pushed the callous thoughts away as best I could, just as I did every other time.

My steps brought me to the main path, which was illuminated with glowing solar lights. The warm radiance guided me in a trail as I studied each booth and every tent. There were numerous snack bars with freshly popped popcorn, soft pretzels, taffy, and warm apple cider. The smells from the stands were nothing short of amazing, and they were the only true form of magic in this carnival. I had to stop myself from getting a treat every time I passed them, even though the temptation was unbearable.

Within the main grounds, there were festival games, little shops, and stages for performances. There was also a tattoo booth, a palm reading station, and an archery setup. Guests could learn the basics of the bow and arrow, get a dagger inked under their skin, or have their future spelled out for them in five minutes.

All the stands were covered in a red and white striped fabric with lamps and twinkle lights glimmering from the inside.

Men on stilts walked past me, people on unicycles made their rounds, and women with light-up hula-hoops danced in the spaces between.

And this was only part of the rehearsal. The week hadn't even begun yet.

It was the week of enchantment, the week of enthrallment, the week of magic.

The week of the *Île de la Revêrie,* also known as *Reverie Island.*

Once a year, a few private planes fly into the hidden island off the coast of France and bring the most exclusive set of guests. They are the highest of the high, the richest of the rich, and usually the scummiest of the scum, and they're welcome here by invite only. The events that occur during the week and the island itself are so completely hush-hush that those who come here are determined to keep the rest of the world out of its secrets.

How they kept us hidden, I wasn't sure. But based on the rumors, the occasional drunken confessions of the guests, and my ability to piece two and two together, I had an idea of how things went *outside* the island, and it wasn't pretty.

But when the time comes and they're actually here, the week finally gives them a chance to let go and abandon their corporate jobs and dark city lives.

Which means we are determined to give them nothing but the best. We put on a damn good show, and that's what brings the same people back every year.

They stay for the entire week, seven days and six nights, with events and acts happening all hours of the day and all throughout the night.

For a week, the *Île de la Rêverie* doesn't sleep.

Guests are given a stay that makes everything worth the trip. They are accommodated with a luxury-style tent with heating and air conditioning, a makeshift, fully stocked kitchen, a full-sized bathroom, and of course, an extravagant bedroom.

But even with a lavish resort-style stay, the guests are presented with only two rules while visiting.

The first rule: no one under eighteen is allowed on the island.

There are too many activities that take place on the island that children are not permitted to be involved in; therefore, not a single underaged human can step foot on Reverie Island.

Although, I was sixteen when I came to the island, making me the lone exception to the rule. I didn't even know the age requirement was a thing until years later when I overheard someone mention it in passing. I questioned Vark about it, and he willingly gave me a straightforward answer.

"I could see it in you, Willa. The moment I found you, I knew you had the drive, the presentation, the look. You had it, *and I'd be damned if I let you slip from between my fingers. And besides,"* his voice was quiet as his eyes raked over my body, *"rules are always meant to be broken."*

That rule was only broken with me and hasn't been broken since.

Then there was the second rule: the performers are off-limits.

Because, as we all know, sometimes guests want to do more than just watch.

Their entitlement back in the real world doesn't transfer to privilege on the island, even though they sometimes think it should. The performers have a job to do and an image to maintain; therefore, any involvement with a guest will have both the performer and the guest removed indefinitely.

Thankfully, the guests respect both the rule and the performers, tending to their own needs with each other in a few available options. Three exclusive tents, the *Onyx, Twyx,* and *Thryx* tents, were dedicated to hidden activities. The activities that take place inside are to be private and remain within those tented walls, and guests are advised to enter at their own risk. Or, if they want even more privacy, they can entertain each other in the comfort of their own luxury tents.

In my time here, everyone mostly stuck to the rules, and there has never been anything *too* extreme involving guests with performers. I experienced a guy grab my ass once, and he was taken away to be thrown in "carny jail" before I could even turn around and see who it was.

No one saw him again that week, and from my understanding, he wasn't invited back for any of the years following.

Vark takes the safety of his employees seriously and treats them respectfully. Even though he runs a strict show and expects the most from us, he always makes it a point to prioritize us and keep the guests in line.

As long as the guests stay in their happy lane, they have everything they could ever want or need on this little island I call home.

When the guests are not on the island, the performers and full-time workers stay here year-round. We keep ourselves busy with things to do in the off-season to prepare for next year's week, such as landscaping, maintenance, and creating new routines. Plus, the basic flights to and from here are so sparse, we don't have any chances to leave. No one ever complains because no one ever wants or needs to go.

To prepare for the week of events and guests, we get a large shipment of last-minute items we need the week *before* the events, and the leftover matter gets flown out the following days after. Clothing, toiletries, and other necessities are shipped in bulk once or twice a year and placed in our storage building. Perishable foods come on either small cargo planes or boats once every three months and are stored in our walk-in freezer until needed.

Basically, we have everything we could ever ask for.

It's our perfect little village.

Well, the word "perfect" might be a stretch.

As I passed by a few employees taking things back to the freezer, a voice called out to me from a nearby tent.

"Willa, sweetheart!"

I stopped and turned to see Troy behind the short viewing glass in his glowing tent, with sweat beading down his temples and his gloved hands covered in a cinnamon sugar mixture.

I shot him a smile, my heart warming at his greeting. "Hi, Troy," I returned his welcome.

Troy was one of the best people I've met on this island. Soon after I arrived, he became like a dad to me—a much younger, friendlier dad—and I loved seeing him in passing when I could. He gave me advice whenever I asked for it, he always made sure I was fed and cared for, and he never went a day without saying hi to me. With his short, pepper-colored hair and light brown eyes, he radiated a comfort I never had prior to coming here.

When I took a step into the tent, I noticed his eyes flash over my dirty sweatpants. His gaze had a subtle look of disappointment, but it only lasted a split second. Pushing it away, he reached under the glass, grabbed a clear bag of cinnamon almonds, and tossed them to me. I caught them easily.

"For you," he said, lifting his shoulder to wipe some lingering sweat away. "I hear you're killing it out there."

A heavy scent of roasted spices wafted in my direction, filling my lungs, and I enjoyed it more than I realized.

I crinkled my nose with a grin that stayed. *"We,"* I corrected.

Troy shook his head. "No. *You.*"

His indication was loud and clear.

I reached into my pocket and dug around for a few dollar bills. The island was cash only, requiring all of us here to comply with a single form of currency. Honestly, it made it easier on us in the end.

Troy raised his gloved hand and shook his head. "No, no. It's on me."

With my cheeks turning a faint shade of red, I held up the almonds. "Thank you."

He gave me a warm smile as I headed out of the tent and back onto the main path. Walking north, I made my way up toward my trailer.

My *home.*

The beautiful *Île de la Revêrie* is shaped like a perfect teardrop. The central grounds of the carnival are located in the southern part of the land, formed along the bottom curve. All of the guests' tents are gathered on the northwestern coast, while all of the employees' and performers' trailers are on the northeastern coast, the two plots separated by a thick wooded forest.

Up toward the tip of the island, once you break out of the woods, there's a large lot of land where we grow some fruits and vegetables. It isn't much and takes more work than what is returned, but it helps when we are between food shipments.

And when you go even farther north, you hit the top of the teardrop, where the land meets the ocean like the tip of an arrow.

Therapia Point.

It's a beautiful scene, especially when you stumble out for the sunset. The golden rays reflect off the shimmering waters, giving it an indigo glow, contrasting perfectly with the vibrant green forestry on the land.

The point also hosts our source of natural freshwater, thanks to a beautiful, hidden waterfall. It's shielded by trees and the hovering cliffs surrounding it, almost giving it the illusion of being in a cave.

The location wasn't a secret by any means, but most people on the island didn't frequent the point unless they needed to make a trip up for water.

I, on the other hand, love to go there whenever I need to get away.

Whoever found this island hit the jackpot because it's so beautiful and effortlessly livable.

When Vark took me under his wing and brought me here, I was nervous at first, as any sixteen-year-old would be. But once I found my footing and became accustomed to the ways of the land, I couldn't see myself anywhere else.

I fell into this fucked up carnival lifestyle, and I wouldn't trade it for anything.

I continued down the stone path until I reached the end. A wooden fence outlined the edge of the public grounds, and I managed to swing my leg over and climb it, nearing my own personal lot.

Everyone who lived here had their own trailer. The workers who lived with their spouses had a bigger trailer to accommodate them. The rest of us, myself included, had a one-person trailer. We were all decently spaced out, with a good-sized plot of land included for each person, and we all had enough privacy to keep us sane.

One thing was true. The trailers were so damn nice.

It was like walking into a small apartment. We had beautiful furniture, a stocked fridge, plumbing, heating and cooling, and everything in between. My bed was the most comfortable bed I've ever laid on, and my shower had *fantastic* water pressure.

Besides Therapia Point, my trailer was the one place I loved to be more than anywhere else. It was my safe space away from the noise, the crowds, and the person who used me.

I walked in, shut the door behind me, and locked it. I threw the almonds on my kitchen counter and unzipped my sweatshirt.

Three loud knocks pounded on my door, causing me to jump and my heart to skip.

"Willa!"

I dropped my shoulders and silently sighed.

"Willa," the voice called to me again, this time in a sing-song tone. "Willa, I know you're in there. I just saw you go in."

The pounding on the door sounded once more. For a moment, I remained still as both my mind and body craved solace. All I wanted to do was shower and get this creamy, sticky liquid off and out of me.

"Don't make me climb in your tiny ass window. You know damn well I can."

That made me smile briefly. I walked to the door and swung it open.

There, looking at me with a sly grin, was my best friend on this island.

Six.

"What are you doing here, Six? Don't you have rehearsal?"

He pushed his way into my trailer and beelined for the fridge. "Rehearsal was *shit*, Willa. It was boring as fuck." He grabbed a bottle of water and motioned it to me, offering it as if *I* were the guest. I shook my head.

"Did you know that Link figured out how to twist and pop both his kneecaps?"

I raised my eyebrows.

"Yeah, I know. I'm so *fucking* jealous. Meanwhile, all I can do is hyperextend like a sad-ass flamingo."

Six was the best contortionist on this island, possibly in the world. He got his name from being a lanky six foot six inches tall and his insane ability to dislocate any six joints from his body at any given time. At the *same* time.

The guy was a walking Rubik's cube, with the ways he could twist and turn and somehow find his way back without a single pulled muscle or permanent injury. Link was the other contortionist here, and contrary to Six's beliefs, he wasn't nearly as good as Six. But together, they freaked people out, and the guests loved it.

People *love* strange and chaotic.

"Hey, you'll never guess what I heard," he began, taking a drink of his water.

I rested my arm over the back of a kitchen chair, staring at him expectantly, waiting for him to elaborate.

He *always* elaborated.

"There's someone new here."

I paused. This was hardly news. "Okay, and?"

"*And*," he leaned forward, his face lit up with glee, "he's a *magician.*"

I narrowed my eyes. *Another magician?* The only magic act on the island was from me and Bram, and we did a damn good job. No one else was needed.

At least, that's what I thought.

"Does Bram know?" I asked Six, who, judging by his wide eyes and tight-lipped grin, looked too invested in this new, juicy gossip. And damn me for giving my first knee-jerk reaction to Bram. I hated the fact that he was the first one I thought about.

Six gave his bony shoulder a shrug. "Fuck if I know. I heard and came straight here."

I groaned. Right now, this was the last thing I wanted to deal with, but there was no way to avoid it.

What was Vark thinking, adding a new act this close to opening? It was one thing to bring in a new act months ahead of time, but it didn't seem wise to bring in someone while the pressure was on. He was going to throw everyone *and* our schedules off. We now had to squeeze another act into the already overflowing list of events.

I could only hope he'd put the newcomer on the overnight shift. That way, we won't cross paths, and there won't be a high demand for magic when Bram and I aren't around.

After Six took another swig of his water, he finally took a second to scan over my clothes. His bleached eyebrows furrowed, and a worried expression flashed across his face.

"Willa, what the hell? Did he—"

"Can we not?" I raised a hand, cutting him off. "I don't want to think about that right now."

Six closed his mouth and leaned back. I could see the fire in his eyes, the anger striking his features, and I knew all he wanted to do was rip Bram a new one. But for now, he had to put me first and accept the fact that I had *no* desire to go there.

We could address it *after* I sorted out this new information.

With a sigh, I headed to my bathroom. "Give me a minute."

Closing myself in, I undressed and cleaned up. I got in the shower long enough to scrub the disgusting liquids that were still seeping out of me and wash away the leftover dirt on my arms and legs. I put on a fresh pair of jeans, a tan sweatshirt, and pulled my hair into a high ponytail.

When I came out of the bathroom, I noticed that Six had already made himself comfortable on my couch and was watching some trashy reality show on TV.

Leave it to him to soak up all the gossip he can, even when he's not involved. I shook my head with a grin as I headed to leave.

"You coming?" I asked, slipping on my shoes at the front door.

Six clicked off the TV and pushed himself off the couch. "Hell yeah. You know I can't miss this shit."

We walked out together while Six pulled out a carton of cigarettes, popped one out, and then offered the box to me. I took one and placed it between my lips.

"What do you think Vark will say?" Six asked as he pulled a lighter out of his pocket and lit both cigarettes.

"To me? Or to Bram?" I clarified, then took a long inhale, savoring the harsh vapor feeling in my lungs. "No matter what, he'll probably give me some bullshit answer like he always does."

Vark was known for being elusive. He would be seen meeting other men, ones I'd never seen before, with their whispers hushed and their lips sealed. If someone asked him about it, he would dismiss it immediately into oblivion.

And that's when we learned that some things just weren't—and will never be—our business.

Even though Vark and his private conversations were always undisclosed, he still held me and Bram to a higher standard on the island. We were the ones that brought in the most money, the happiest guests, and the highest compliments.

But even in all our praise, Vark seemed to favor Bram more than me, and I could never figure out why.

Thankfully, I was never truly bothered by the undeniable bias.

But what *did* bother me was the fact that Vark knew how Bram could be and did nothing about it.

Nobody ever did anything about it.

Side by side, Six and I walked and smoked until we came to Vark's office. He had a permanent building that doubled as his house. It was big, bigger than anyone else's place, but it was used for more than just a living space. All business was conducted there, along with any first-aid that may be needed and the storage of minor inventories.

The house was a tan, two-story structure with beautiful glass French doors along the bottom. The doors were curtained with cream, opaque shades, and the only thing I could see inside was the orangish-yellow glow of a tabletop lamp.

"Wait here," I whispered to Six, dropping the butt of my cigarette and squashing it with my shoe.

"Come on," Six whined, and the sound grated the inside of my ears. "I'm nosey."

I rolled my eyes at his obsessive need. "Then press your ear to the door. But don't make yourself known."

"Fine."

Hesitantly, I approached the large glass doors and knocked on the frame.

A brief laugh, then a cough, echoed through the glass. After a beat, I knocked again.

"Come on in," Vark's distinguishable voice called out.

I pushed open the door to the living room, where Vark sat in one of his leather lounge chairs, facing me. He held a cigar between the short fingers that also clutched a glass of whiskey.

Another person sat in the lounge chair across from him, and even though he was facing away from me, there was no mistaking who it was.

"Bram?" I asked, and he looked over his shoulder at me.

A small piece of me was hurt at the fact that he was already here, probably getting valuable information about the newcomer without me.

Then again, how could I be upset when I came here without finding him first?

"My little *magic rabbit,*" he said with an egotistical grin and matching wink. I forced myself to hide the grimace that was trying to claw its way out of me.

"I'm assuming you heard?" Vark asked, even though it was phrased as more of a statement than a question.

"Word spreads fast around here, Vark. You know that," Bram added before I could get a word in.

"Of course," Vark confirmed. "But I didn't expect her to show up until morning."

"Can someone tell me what's going on?" I asked, stepping closer to them, making my presence known.

Vark gave a meaty shrug. "I hired another magician. Since you guys bring in the biggest audience and have the highest reviews, I figured another show wouldn't hurt. More revenue, more interaction, happy customers, am I right?"

Obviously, he *was* right, but I didn't answer that.

"Did *you* find him?" I inquired, my voice hindered by a thin layer of nervousness.

"Yes," Vark answered.

Once, sometimes twice a year, Vark makes it a point to fly to another part of the world to scout for new acts. Where he goes, no one knows until he gets back.

Sometimes, he brings someone back with him, and sometimes, he comes back alone. He never brings someone he feels may be subpar, or someone with too many strings attached to their previous life, because whoever comes here stays here. Everyone who is presented with the job opportunity and willingly accepts it must also agree to live the rest of their life here. The island is too exclusive for anyone to leave.

Most of the time, the people Vark finds are too desperate to start over to care about the logistics of the island.

I know I was.

I looked to Bram, who returned my gaze and gave an effortless nod of his head. "Come on, you know we're the best and always will be."

His eyes sparkled under the dim lights of the office, and I couldn't help but stare at the reddish hue flushing his cheeks. I hated the way his face glowed because I knew it was the result of his forced orgasm in me only an hour ago.

And I hated the way he could get hard again instantly if he wanted to.

His voice snapped me out of my untimely animosity. "Do you feel threatened?"

There was a small hesitation, one that wanted to spark a new anxious life in me, but I shook it away. "No," I responded quietly.

"Good," Bram spoke confidently, his slick eyes still on me. "There's nothing to worry about. I bet this guy is a loser, anyway."

Vark cut in. "Actually, he's not. Not at all. He's incredible."

Bram and I froze, our bodies stock-still, and our heads turned to look at Vark as he leaned forward.

"I wouldn't hire someone who couldn't bring this place up another level. Especially not this close to opening."

My heartbeat sped up slightly. Vark didn't disagree with Bram when he said we were the best, but he *did* imply that the newcomer might be just as promising.

But what did I have to worry about? I've been here since I was sixteen, and the thought of leaving or losing my position had never crossed my mind. I've always felt secure in my life here.

So, why does this feel off?

Illusion

Why do I feel like this is going to change everything?

"In fact…" Vark began, looking at his watch. It was just past sundown, rehearsals were wrapping up, and everyone was closing for the night. In less than thirty minutes, everyone would be back in their trailers until morning.

Vark's anticipation could only mean one thing.

Two gentle knocks tapped on the glass door, and Bram quickly jumped to his feet and stepped beside me. I ignored his presence as Vark slowly walked past us and to the door. He opened it, revealing exactly who he was expecting.

"Dresden. You made it."

3

The man standing at the open door nodded to Vark, then instantly made eye contact with me. He was tall, with the strap of his duffel bag slung over his broad shoulder and the top of his head almost reaching the height of the doorframe.

Six, who looked to be only about two inches taller than Dresden, slid into the open space behind him. He quickly and not-so-subtly pointed to him as he made direct eye contact with me.

"It's him," he silently mouthed to me.

Vark caught on instantly. "Six, get the fuck outta here."

"Yes, sir." With that, Six scrambled off. I give it an hour—maybe two if I'm lucky—until he returns to my trailer, begging for more information.

Dresden watched him leave, his head turned over his shoulder, his gaze following the path of his exit.

Then he turned his sight back to us.

More specifically, to *me*.

Holy shit.

His ice-blue eyes met mine, and for the first time in what felt like forever, I didn't feel like I was being assessed. His look was casual but powerful, calm yet intense.

Bram must've noticed my lingering stare because he immediately wrapped his arm around my waist, and I could feel my insides recoil. Dresden's eyes briefly moved to the new hand on my hip before turning back to Vark, his face expressionless.

"Welcome to *Île de la Revêrie*, Dresden," Vark said, opening his arms and allowing Dresden to step through the threshold.

Bram leaned close to my ear in a whisper, and it physically pained me to not move away. "What the fuck kind of name is *Dresden?*"

Dresden must have heard him because, without looking, he replied. "Dres is fine."

"Dres?" Bram sneered, a disgusted look filling his features.

With a quick jab, I sent my elbow into Bram's side, hoping by some miracle he would shut up. He did, and by some *other* miracle, he also dropped his hand from my waist. He's surrounded by people named *"Six"* and *"Vark,"* yet he dares to call out someone's uncommon name? I couldn't help but roll my eyes.

"How was your flight?" Vark asked, even though it was evident by the insincere tone that he didn't care. Vark practically had dollar bills painted on his eyeballs, and small talk was at the bottom of his interests.

"Fine," Dres replied, shrugging it off. It seemed like he didn't care about small talk, either.

"Need a drink?"

"No."

Vark took another puff of his cigar and headed back to his chair. "Well, this is my office. If you need anything, you come here. If I'm not around, just call or text me, and I'll meet you here."

Dres gave him a single nod in acknowledgement, causing a lock of his smooth, dark hair to fall over his forehead. I watched as he slicked it back with one fluid, mindless movement.

"This is Bram and Willa," Vark extended a hand toward us. "They are the main magic act here. They have the primetime slot, as you're aware."

Dres said nothing as his eyes moved back to mine, not bothering to spare even half a glance at Bram. A single dark freckle rested under the center of his right eye, and I tried not to grin at the little identification marker.

"You have the overnight slot. You'll get a good crowd, some stragglers, some drunks, but I'm sure you can handle that."

Once again, Dres remained silent.

"Your first rehearsal is tomorrow afternoon. The Spider Tent at 4 PM."

Dres kept his eyes on me as Bram crossed his arms over his chest. I could feel Bram's body grow tense next to me at the simple fact that Dres didn't care about him or the blatant intimidation he was trying to convey.

"Bram and Willa will show you to your place." Vark turned to us. "He's in Lot 22. Make sure he gets in and settled."

Vark tossed a set of keys to Dres, who caught them without breaking eye contact with me.

I shifted uncomfortably, unable to take the heat of his stare off of me, even if I wasn't returning the eye contact. I looked to Vark, my feet, and anywhere else in the room. But his eyes felt like a sword to the stomach, the blade slicing me and stiffening every muscle in my body.

Then, without warning, my skin turned cold. Literal shivers covered me, creating a surface of goosebumps everywhere on my body.

What the hell?

I was freezing and on the verge of trembling, and *that's* when I finally looked back at Dres.

There was only the beat of a moment before he dropped his eyes and turned back to the door, heading out without a word.

Illusion

Bram and I followed with quick steps, and Vark shut the door behind us.

The second we made it outside, my frozen skin warmed, and I no longer had goosebumps.

Was I imagining things? Simply meeting Dres shouldn't have that big of an effect on me.

Right?

Bram turned to me and snipped his words out, oblivious to my unprovoked chills. "Willa, let's go. He can find the place himself."

Dres kept his steady stride ahead, about three paces in front of us. We all found ourselves back on the main stone path, and when I didn't respond, Bram clutched my elbow.

"Willa."

"I'll be fine," Dres cut in without looking back to us.

Bram raised his eyebrows in a told-you-so look, silently noting that Dres just agreed. He'll be *fine.*

I shook my head.

"Bram, don't be a dick. It's his first day here. The least we could do is show him where he lives."

"Whatever," he scoffed as he turned his shoulders away. "I'm fucking starving anyway. I'll see you tomorrow."

Without a proper goodbye, Bram jogged away and headed toward the line of food tents. I turned the opposite way to catch up to Dres, who was farther up the path.

"Hey," I said, slightly out of breath. "Sorry. He's not—"

"Don't," Dres cut off, not bothering to look at me. He kept his hand gripped on the strap of the duffle bag over his shoulder.

I narrowed my eyes. "Don't what?"

Dres ignored me and kept walking.

Okay, what the fuck was his deal?

I brushed off the quick dismissal and tried to give him the benefit of the doubt. Maybe he was nervous, or maybe he needed time to adjust to being in a new place.

I knew what it was like feeling overwhelmed with a big change.

From the side of my vision, I glanced to him. His eyes looked haunted, like he had a story that needed to be told. There was something about him, something hidden, something buried.

Something broken.

"So," I started, trying again as I inhaled. I pulled a pack of cigarettes from my back pocket and picked one out. "How did you end up here?" The question was caught in a mumble as I lit the end of the stick and inhaled.

Dres glanced over at me, his eyes darting down to the smoke between my lips, then back up to my eyes before moving away.

There was that broken look again.

"Do you want one?" I asked, holding the carton out to him.

"No." His answer was abrupt, and I took that as a clear sign to put the pack away. Either he didn't like smoking, he was trying to quit, or he just didn't like me.

Maybe all of the above.

We walked side by side around the edge of the grounds until we reached the back of the tents. As nightfall reached the horizon, lights from the main area began turning off, and I knew everyone was done for the day.

I took this small opportunity to wiggle my way into a cracked opening of his trust.

"Let me show you something," I spoke quietly, dropping the leftover cigarette to the ground and crushing it with my shoe.

Dres looked to me expectantly, and I nodded off to the side.

"There's a back way to the lots. It's a shortcut. When you're tired—*which you will be*—this way will be a lifesaver."

Dres followed as I took him to the wooden fences that lined the property. Hopping over, he did the same, and we walked down a quiet, worn path that cut between hidden lots. It was in no way a secret, but it wasn't the path that everyone else took. Some nights, it was a nice little escape away from everyone.

"I'm in Lot 11, which means you're behind me and to the left a bit."

Illusion

We walked past my trailer, which was quiet and dark inside. I was surprised that Six wasn't sitting on my front step, waiting for me and any information I had to give, but I knew he would show up eventually.

Cutting through my spacious lawn, I led him back to his trailer. Lot 22.

It was just like everyone else's. White siding, grey door, two stone steps to the inside. Placing my hands on my hips, I looked at the window that—if it was the same floorplan as mine—peered into the living room.

And before I could say another word, before I could welcome him here and into this new world, he unlocked the door, stepped inside, and shut it behind him.

Okay. You're welcome, asshole.

I rolled my eyes, turned away, and headed back to my trailer, hoping this new prick wasn't anything like the one I already worked with.

4

Stepping out of the coffin box, I grabbed Bram's sweaty palm and struck a pose. Not a single sword caught on my black-shaping bodysuit this time, thankfully. This one was expensive.

Our act was perfect. Our timing was spot on. Our stage presence was undeniable.

Not a single flaw.

At least, that's what I thought until my eyes locked on Dres sitting in the audience, his face bored, his eyes tired. He was leaning back with his knees open and his chin resting in the palm of his hand.

He looked so unimpressed.

Vark stood off to the side, propped against one of the tent poles. "Good. Time's up."

I wasted no time dropping Bram's hand, hurrying off to the side of the stage, and pulling on my sweatpants. Bram followed close behind and smacked my ass as he passed me. "Good job, *magic rabbit.*"

I swatted his hand away and scoffed.

"Dres, you're up." Vark's voice boomed through the empty seats and echoed onto the stage. Behind-the-scenes workers cleared out our set to make room for the next act, and I could hear Dres get up from his seat. I quickly pulled a light grey sweatshirt over my head, tucked my hair back into a messy ponytail, and hopped off stage.

"Do you have an assistant?" Vark asked, his phlegmy voice booming as he stood alongside the striped walls of the tent.

"No."

"Why not?"

Dres headed up toward the stage, eyeing me as he passed me. He blinked his icy eyes in my direction, his face remaining expressionless as he answered.

"Don't need one."

I furrowed my eyebrows and watched as he effortlessly climbed up on the stage with his backwards baseball hat, white t-shirt, and ripped jeans, making him look like nothing more than an ordinary street performer.

Instead of heading out of the tent, I made my way into one of the middle rows and sat down. I wanted to get an idea of what Dres' act was like, what kind of style he had, and if he was as entertaining as Vark made him out to be.

Last night, I stayed up until midnight texting Six about Dres. Six wanted to know everything, but I had nothing to tell him. There was minimal interaction and hardly any conversation between us. It was disappointing for Six, to say the least.

The warm lights dimmed, and I sat back in my seat.

Dres lifted a hand, turning it both ways to show he wasn't hiding anything.

He also lifted his forearms, showing the hypothetical audience that there was no way he could be concealing anything while wearing a simple white t-shirt.

Of course, it *looked* like nothing to the untrained eye, but I knew something was waiting to come out of the shadows.

He lifted his other hand, doing the same. Nothing to see, nothing to hide.

He turned around, showing his back to me and Vark, his hands still lifted in a ninety-degree angle.

And then his hands caught on fire.

My heart skipped a small beat as the flames spread down his forearms and to his elbows, but I knew there was an easy explanation for this. He was wearing a fake, flammable skin, one that resembled tight, fleshy gloves. A tap of his shoe on the floor pressed a button that ignited the flame.

But then he turned around, and with a slow, steady swipe of his hand, the flame went out on one arm. He mirrored the other side, and I could see the burn marks on his skin. They were fresh, they were oozing, they were raw.

That doesn't happen with fake skin.

When fake skin is set on fire, it looks perfectly normal when the flames are gone.

Right now, he looks like he should be in pain. He looks like he should be heading straight to a hospital.

I sat forward in my seat as he continued on with his show, as if he wasn't just burning himself alive. His face was stoic, expressionless, and concentrated. His light eyes blinked slowly, painfully, as he looked down at his injured skin.

Holy shit.

Moving his arms back down, he cautiously moved his hand outward. Lifting his burnt index finger, he pointed to the floor, sending a small ball of fire down onto the stage.

Okay, another easy explanation. He has a small, clear tube on the inside of his finger that can't be seen from this far away. He can activate it with another click of a button, sending a lit ball of something—*anything*—flammable to the floor.

But in the short amount of time it took me and Bram to get off the stage and for Dres to get on, I didn't see any setup. I didn't see any stagehands helping him with equipment, placements, or anything.

He simply climbed up and started his act.

Illusion

The small fire remained lit on the stage floor. I glanced over to Vark, who seemed to be entranced by the whole thing, like he was thinking the same thought as me.

This seemed real. Almost too real.

But that was the point of a magic act, right? We all wanted to make the viewer think it *wasn't* just an illusion. We wanted people to believe in the magic.

He was doing an awfully good job of it so far.

Damn it.

In a split second, the fire spread around him in a perfect circle.

Easy. Whatever was flammable was also placed on the floor around him before the show.

It could be anything, like a thin layer of gasoline, acetone, or anything flammable. Maybe it was there before my show, and I just didn't realize it. I promised myself I would pay more attention next time.

But then, with a quick snap of his burnt fingers, the fire completely vanished.

Okay, so there was someone else controlling the fire. I gave the idea a mental shrug. We have people do that for our act sometimes, too. It's definitely not uncommon to have magic controlled off-stage for some illusions.

But then Dres lifted his finger, the same one he used to point at the floor, and motioned to Vark.

"Lift your hand," Dres spoke softly and calmly across the stage.

Vark did as he was told and lifted his hand palm up. The instant his hand was parallel to the floor, Vark's palm flared with a bright orange flame. Vark quickly dropped his hand to his leg, extinguishing the flame in a brief panic.

So, Vark was in on this, too?

I cinched my eyebrows, confused. It was unlike Vark to be part of any act, especially when someone was new and trying to gain traction in their performance. He always had too much going on to commit to taking part in a show.

Vark continued to bat out the flame as I looked back to Dres, who was already staring at me. I swallowed any new hesitancy and watched his next move.

He brought his burnt finger up as he opened his mouth. Dropping his tongue down, he pointed to the center of it, then slowly trailed it down to the tip, all while never breaking eye contact with me.

What was he doing? What did this mean?

And then I felt it.

A stabbing pain ran down the surface of my tongue, and I immediately covered my mouth with my hand. Reactive tears welled in my eyes at the sudden burning sensation.

Dres pulled his tongue back in his mouth, a subtle, coy smile playing on his lips as he watched my quick dismay.

I sprang up from my seat, ran out of my row, and bolted to the back exit of the tent. I needed water, and I needed it fast.

I ran directly to Troy's tent, dodging and avoiding everyone along the way. The second I burst into the entrance, his eyes found mine. A new worry etched into his tone. "Darlin', you okay?"

"Water," I rasped out, and he immediately grabbed a bottle from under his display case. I opened it and chugged the contents, the cold liquid soothing the intensity on my tongue.

"Willa, what's goin' on?"

I drank about half the bottle before taking a breath. "I don't know. I don't... I don't get it."

"Get what?" Troy leaned forward on the glass case, worried.

I shook my head. "Troy, if I even knew how to explain—"

My words were cut off by the numbness in my tongue and the loss of my breath, forcing me to take another drink.

Placing the cap back on, I let out a deep exhale. "I burnt my tongue. That's all."

A heavy pause lingered in the air. "Alright, alright," Troy said as he leaned back, knowing I wasn't giving him the whole truth. With a few understanding pats on the glass, he motioned to the bottle of water in my hands. "Don't worry, it's on me."

"Thank you," I said through another breath, taking the drink with me as I walked away.

Going back the way I came, I found myself nearing The Spider Tent. Of course, part of me wanted to see the rest of the magic act, but the other part of me didn't want to step foot back in there while he was performing.

What just happened—*what he did to me*—could not be explained.

That wasn't magic. That was something else.

Voodoo? Witchcraft? Black magic?

Instead of going back in, my anxious steps paced along the stone path in front of the tent. My stride was light, my breathing was heavy, and my mind was racing. All I could think about was the feeling I had in my mouth, the way his finger ran down his *own* tongue, and the way his eyes watched *me* the whole time.

After about an hour, I heard rustling coming from the tent entrance. Vark opened the thick tarp, allowing Dres through first. Vark let out a deep, rumbled laugh next to a healed, calm, and relaxed Dres.

I froze.

Vark was *laughing?* After what just happened?

I stood there stunned, confused, and unable to understand how he went from that… to this.

Vark gave Dres' shoulders a jostle, then headed in the opposite direction, back toward his office.

"Hey, I'll see ya tomorrow, Big Guy!"

Dres gave a courteous nod but didn't give any sort of expression—no smile, no wave, nothing. His face remained blank as he walked in my direction en route to his trailer.

I remained still, half expecting him to stop and talk to me or to apologize for burning me.

But he didn't.

He kept walking, passing by me without a single glance my way, wearing his white t-shirt, his faded, ripped jeans, and his dirty Vans.

It was like I was invisible.

"Hey," I turned and called out to him as he walked further away.

He didn't stop. He didn't respond.

"Hey!" This time, I shouted louder and ran to catch up to him. There was no way I was letting him go without any sort of explanation.

I caught up to his side, matching his pace as I glared at him. He didn't bother to look over at me.

"What *the hell* was that?" I asked, motioning back to The Spider Tent.

Dres gave a fraction of a furrowed brow, but it was so subtle that it could've been from anything. A speck of dirt in his eye. A pinch of a headache in his skull. An ache in his foot that he was just now noticing. Whatever it was, he paid it—*and me*—no mind as he continued on.

"Hello?" I pushed. I waved a hand in front of his face, but he ignored it. "I'm *talking to you,*" I said with a bite as I snapped my fingers only inches from his nose. It was then that Dres finally gave a side glance in my direction. His cold eyes met with mine, flashing me a look of unwanted heat, and suddenly, I wasn't angry with him anymore.

I just wanted the truth.

I dropped my hand, and he turned back to the path in front of him.

Obviously, I wasn't going to let this go. I needed an explanation.

"What you did back there," I started, keeping up with his stride, "it was almost like it was…"

I struggled to find an appropriate word. I needed something that wasn't too outrageous and not too obscure.

"…Real?" Dres answered for me, and I found myself startled by his deep voice.

That was the word I wanted to use, yes, but we all know that wasn't real. Everyone, *especially me,* knows magic isn't real. It's all an illusion; it's just the execution that people find magical.

"No," I quipped. But after fallen moments without any other words and no easy explanation, I changed my answer. "I mean, I guess, yeah," I responded, and Dres didn't bat an eye.

It's like he expected this from me.

"Was it?" I asked.

He kept walking and didn't answer.

I asked again. "Was it real?"

With a quick exhale, Dres pressed his lips together briefly before answering. "If you're asking me that, doesn't that mean I'm doing my job correctly?"

I stopped in my tracks, knowing he was right.

And oddly enough, he stopped walking, too. He watched me as I tried to answer him in my mind, turning my attempted words with a baffled twist, coming at the resolution from every angle.

And I came up short because, with every honest bone in my body, I couldn't tell if his act was real or not.

When he realized I wasn't going to give him a verbal answer, he started walking again, and I followed.

"What did Vark think of your show?" I asked, trailing his path.

Dres shrugged. "Fine."

Fine? That was it? Just… Fine?

I inhaled a deep breath, trying to keep my composure at his cagey answers. He was *not* making this easy.

"Do you think you're ready for the big week?" I asked.

"Sure," he replied.

Sure.

"It's only two weeks away," I assured, and he remained silent.

I rolled my eyes, feeling the need for some type of information creep up and into my throat. God, it was like talking to a brick wall. An annoyingly dense, tall, broody brick wall.

I held up the bottle of water I had received from Troy and shook it, making the last of the water splash inside the plastic. "Thanks for this, by the way."

A subtle look of confusion slipped into his expression as he eyed the bottle.

"I had to get this after you… you know."

Dres cocked an eyebrow. "You think *that's* what gave you relief?"

Now, it was my turn to look puzzled. *What?* What was he implying?

"What do you mean?" I asked, but he ignored my need for clarification.

I let the bottle fall to my side as we neared the wooden fence. I climbed over first, and Dres followed suit, his long legs effortlessly twisting him to the other side. He took a few more steps toward our trailers and spoke up.

"How much do I owe you?" he asked, motioning to the bottle with his eyes.

I looked down at the plastic.

Technically, nothing. "Four dollars," I lied.

Dres stopped walking and locked eyes with me, not a blink or flicker of his bright irises. His stare was deep, planting a set of unspoken roots in my chest. I held his gaze, anxiously anticipating his next action.

After a heavy moment, he gave a single nod, then continued to his trailer.

I remained on the worn path as I watched him approach his front door. He reached for the handle, stopping on the step leading up to it.

"Four dollars," he confirmed. "Consider it done." He motioned to me with a dip of his chin, his eyes falling to my left hip. I followed his gaze down to my left side, glancing at the water bottle in my hand, confused about what he meant.

He went inside and shut the door behind him.

Four dollars. *Great.* Good to know he's the type of person who holds himself accountable and pays his dues.

Or maybe he isn't. I don't know anything about this guy other than the fact that he's incredibly baffling.

Brushing it off, I stepped inside my trailer, dropped the water bottle on the counter, and made my way to the bathroom. What I needed right now was a hot, steamy shower and a full night's sleep.

Illusion

As I stripped off my sweatpants, I felt something padded in my left pocket. Sure enough, after shoving my hand inside, I found four folded one-dollar bills.

My heart plummeted to my toes.

There's no way.

There's no *fucking* way.

I dropped them on the floor instantly.

5

"He's good. He's *really* good," I whispered to Six, who was eating this whole thing up. He took a quick sip of his drink, then pulled out a cigarette and lit it.

"Want one?" he asked. I nodded and took one, pushing it between my lips as he lit it for me. I inhaled.

I explained everything that happened with Dres to Six, and he grinned the entire time. Of course, I had to leave out the fact that a small—*very small*—piece of me considered it to be *real* magic, only because I knew it would sound crazy. And the last thing I wanted was a rumor floating around that I, the assistant to a magician, believed magic was *real.*

That was one sure-fire way to make myself into a joke.

"It's like he doesn't even have to try," I explained, holding the cigarette between my fingers. We sat together on an empty picnic bench, watching the workers in their tents get ready for opening. The potent scent of hot, buttered popcorn wafted over to us, mixing with the sweet smell of cinnamon from Troy's tent. I savored the rich aroma, letting it fill the depths of my lungs, opting for the delicious scent rather than the chemical cigarette stench.

"Maybe he just has that gift," Six chimed in, lifting his thin arm in a shrug.

"Like you?" I asked, nudging him.

He nodded in return. "Some things you just can't fake, babe."

"Willa?" A voice sounded to my left. I exhaled leftover smoke and turned to look.

It was Bram.

"Can I talk to you for a minute?"

I didn't even have to look at Six to feel the roll of his eyes. Hesitantly, I nodded and climbed off the picnic bench. Bram led us back to the path, far enough away from Six and still out of the way from the constant buzz of the rest of the carnival. Bram stood to face me, his brown, shoulder-length hair tied back in a low bun, his dark eyes piercing mine, and his expression holding something I hadn't seen before.

Was that... *hesitation?*

"You went to his show last night?" He was asking for my confirmation.

I nodded. "Yeah. How did you know?" I dropped the butt of my cigarette and squashed it under my shoe.

"Vark mentioned it. He's been raving about it all fucking morning." His hand moved to the back of his neck, his palm rubbing the skin almost raw. "Was it really that good?"

With a slow, unsure blink, I let a new uncertainty filter between us. Yes, it was good, but it was good in the sense that it was unexplainable. I couldn't tell Bram that it was captivating or that I was intrigued from the moment Dres stepped on the stage.

Bram would lose his shit.

All Bram wanted was to be the best. And if Dres is here, Bram is going to have to work harder for once.

I glanced over Bram's shoulder, unable to make eye contact with him. "It was alright."

He hissed out a sigh, locking both his hands behind his neck. "Shit, Willa. Don't fuck with me. Are we going to lose our spot?"

"What? No. Why would you think that?"

"It just doesn't feel right."

It took everything in me to not scoff in his face. *Feel right.* Okay. I've told him that his dick doesn't feel right when he jams it in me dry and ignores my cries for him to stop.

I had no sympathy for his worries at that moment, but I knew where he was coming from.

Because he wasn't wrong.

None of this felt right, even though I only saw a sliver of Dres' performance. He was good, definitely better than us, and once people got word of his act, I knew our time slots were in danger of switching. Dres would get prime time, and Bram and I would fall into the overnight slot.

It was inevitable.

But I didn't let the danger show in my expression.

With his hands still clasped together at the base of his head, Bram puffed out his cheeks and blew out a large exhale.

"Bram, it's fine," I reassured. "There won't be enough people watching his overnight show for him to gain popularity."

"All it takes is one person, Willa." He dropped his hands only to raise a single finger at me. *"One person* on night one can spread the word like wildfire."

Once again, he wasn't wrong.

I stared at him in silence, undecided about what else to say or give him to reassure him of something *I* wasn't even sure of.

"Come with me," he pleaded. "Come with me to his rehearsal. We need to see what we're up against."

Memories of last night flashed in my head.

The fire.

The burning.

Dres' wicked grin.

I immediately shook my head. "No. You go. Tell me what you think afterward."

"Willa, please. It's you and me." His hands reached for me with trembling fingers. I've never seen this side of him before. He seemed... desperate.

"We have to make sure we're secure."

Normally, I wouldn't mind watching someone else's act. I've done it hundreds of times before, whether it was to check someone out or to support a friend. I've done it alone, and I've done it with others, including Bram. People have watched our act, as well.

It was a normal thing to do.

But right now, in this moment, my body, mind, and soul were all screaming for me not to go. I didn't want to face Dres again, especially after what happened at his last rehearsal.

I wasn't scared of him, no. That wasn't it. I was apprehensive.

I was filled with a feeling I couldn't place. Two strings I couldn't tie together. A drop of oil and a drop of water that I couldn't mix.

"I already saw it, Bram. I don't need to see it again."

Without warning, Bram reached down and grabbed my hand. He pulled me off the path and into a hidden patch of woods next to the trailers. It was easily out of sight from everyone. Out of the corner of my eye, I could see Six stand to his feet, ready to save me if I needed it. I looked to him and shook my head, silently telling him to stay put. I could handle this on my own.

I always do.

"Willa, now, more than ever, we need to stick together," he voiced. "We need to look like a team."

He dropped my hand, and I instantly crossed my arms over my chest. "A team, Bram? Fuck off. You don't see me as a teammate. You only see me as a release."

"Oh, cut the dramatic shit, Willa. That's not fucking true, and you know it. You and I, we're the best when we perform together. We have a flow that comes naturally."

I paused, slightly annoyed that he was kind of right. But of all the years I've been with him, I've never heard him speak like this. There was a slight quiver in his voice, one that could only be heard if listening for it specifically. He was trying to convince *me* of this when, in reality, he needed to convince *himself.*

Tilting my head, I stared at him. His pupils dilated under the shade of the trees, and I felt myself falter by a fraction. His words held weight to me, and I liked hearing him talk positively about us for once.

Even with the impending dread looming over me, I found a hint of solace in his unconvincing words.

"Now, you're going with me to the rehearsal, and we're going to see it for ourselves."

And we're right back to where we started.

Any comfort I gained from his prior statements was erased the second he dropped his tone with me.

"I'm not going, Bram."

Without hesitation, Bram grabbed my biceps and pushed me up against the nearest tree. The leaves shook above me, scattering shadows on both of us. The crazed look in his eye only intensified as his fingers dug past my sleeves and into my arms. Bram lowered his face into the side of my neck, his breath hot on the thin skin.

"Don't make this hard, Willa…"

He pressed his hips into mine, and I could feel his dick through both of our jeans.

"…even though I already am."

I squeezed my eyes shut. I've been through this exact scenario with him hundreds of times, but never like this. He's only ever taken advantage of me after shows and performances when his high was at its highest and his excitement overtook all other emotions.

This was different.

He was chasing a different type of adrenaline. He was climbing up the ladder of his anxiety and stress, and he was using me to do it.

Letting go of one of my arms, I felt instant relief from his grip as he moved his hand to the front of my jeans. I used my free arm to shove against his chest, but he caught himself before he could stumble. He slipped his warm hand down between my skin and my denim, inching closer to the place where he didn't belong. I tried to grab his wrist and pull it out, but he was too strong. He slid one finger in, swirling in my natural wetness.

"Mmm," he hummed against my neck. "I love it when you're ready for me."

My efforts to kick and push him away were futile. He was taller, stronger, and more resilient than me, and arguing with him would do nothing but incite him to try harder.

"Get the fuck off me, Bram," I bit out through a tightly clenched jaw. "Or I'll scream."

"That wouldn't be a very smart thing to do, *magic rabbit*," he whispered as he slid another finger in.

I wished the feeling of his touch felt good. In fact, time and time again, I tried to trick my mind into believing I liked it just so I could endure the agony of his force.

The sound of his zipper barely registered in my ears as I felt his body shimmy his jeans down to his knees. I continued to squirm under his grasp, but his grip was too tight on me.

There's no way he wasn't leaving bruises.

With swift ease, he unbuttoned my jeans and yanked them down.

"Scream once, and I'll get you off this island so fucking fast you won't know up from down."

Slipping one hand between my legs, he shoved my thighs apart. I didn't fight it anymore. I didn't say anything because I knew his threat was real. He had an unfair pull on this island, and I didn't dare test it. He was close with Vark, closer to him than anyone else, and one conversation between the two of them could change my life.

Plus, it didn't help that I was easily replaceable. Any woman could hop on stage, learn the tricks, and become a magician's assistant. It wasn't rocket science.

I wanted to be here. I loved it here. Over the span of seven years, these people have become my family. They've consoled me in my lows; they've celebrated with me in my highs. The island brought a comfort that I didn't dare risk losing.

So, I pressed my lips into a thin line and let Bram shove himself inside me.

I hated the fact that I said yes to him the first time. I hated the fact that this was completely consensual at one point.

I hated the fact that I thought I meant something to him in the beginning. I thought he wanted me and not just my body. I thought we had something more than just a showmance. I thought wrong, and I hated it all.

As Bram shoved his hips up into mine, he panted his hot breath against my shoulder. "Holy shit, Willa, I love when you squeeze me."

A glisten of a tear rested on the rim of my eyelid at his statement. He thought I was gripping him in pleasure, but in actuality, my body was fighting against him. I was trying to expel him.

With my gaze out of focus and lingering over Bram's shoulder, I noticed a blur along the tree line. A still, dark figure was waiting between the shade of the trees and the sunlit path.

I blinked once, twice, three times before my eyes absorbed the tears that didn't fall and cleared my vision.

It was Dres.

He was half-turned to us, as if he was strolling by and caught us, dressed in a plain black t-shirt and black jeans. His eyes locked onto mine, his expressionless gaze heating the apples of my cheeks as Bram continued to thrust into me.

Dres' eyes moved quickly to Bram's backside, where he scanned him from shoulder to shoulder, from neck to bare ass.

The humiliation I felt in that moment was unlike anything I had ever felt before. The fact that he saw us, saw the look of resentment on my face, and noticed that I wasn't strong enough to fight back was something I'll never get over. I wanted to fall into a puddle on the ground, only to never get back up again.

But I locked my knees and kept myself up.

Then Dres' eyes moved back to mine, the lack of expression remaining, and my skin felt like it had turned to ice. Goosebumps ran down the tops of my arms and legs at his awareness. A pinprick feeling settled at the back of my neck, and I could feel my spine twist in a chill.

And then, as fast as he appeared, he walked away.

"Damn, magic rabbit, I'm that good, huh? I give you goosebumps?"

Dres and his notice were the only things keeping me from punching Bram in the throat at his narcissism. Thankfully, it only took a few more pumps before he unloaded in me and pulled out, putting me out of my temporary misery. The feeling of his cum slipping out and onto the inside of my thigh instantly churned my stomach, so I pulled my jeans and underwear all the way off, used the black cotton panties to wipe myself dry, and then went commando as I pulled my jeans back on.

"Is that for me?" Bram asked with a sadistic smile, reaching for the underwear.

I pulled my hand back and cinched my eyebrows in disgust. "No." I balled up the slime-coated underwear and pushed past him, heading out of the hidden pocket of the woods.

"I'll see you at The Spider Tent in twenty," Bram shouted to me, and I could hear his satisfied grin through his words.

He was getting what he wanted. He always did.

"You're not sitting by this piece of shit alone, you got it?" Six spoke as he wrapped an arm around me, towering high above as he squeezed my shoulders. I nodded with a hint of a smirk as we sauntered toward the tent. I was in no rush to get to Dres' show, and if I was late, too bad.

There was nothing wrong with Six's comfort, besides the fact that I didn't want it. I ached to rip my skin off at his touch—*anyone's touch*—and all I wanted to do was burrow in my bed and sleep until morning. I wanted everyone to leave me alone, and after the big upcoming week at the carnival, hiding away was *exactly* what I planned on doing.

I loved Six, I really did. When I first came to the island, he had already been here a few years. He showed me the ropes, the secrets, the shortcuts, and he was the one who introduced me to Therapia Point. On the night before my very first performance, the night before the guests arrived and the island came to life, he led the way to the top of the teardrop. I had known about the waterfall since it was crucial to everyone's survival, but I had no reason to actually head up there.

Six changed that.

Illusion

The moment my eyes spotted the beautiful falls and the comforting setting around it, I fell in love. It became a place I went to when I needed to think, or stop thinking.

It was a place I could steady myself, where I could ground myself, and where I could escape from the noise of the activities.

It also became a place where I could escape from the horrors of always being watched, wanted, and taken advantage of.

Because when I come here, I always come here alone.

After Six brought me to Therapia Point for the first time, he never came with me again. He knew I connected with the atmosphere in a way that would only be ruined with another person around.

I loved that he understood me without having to talk about it.

Without a doubt, he was my best friend here, and he never failed to make me smile. He always knew when to protect me and when to let me fight for myself.

But right now, I just wanted to be alone. I wanted to go to the point and be alone.

After Bram fucked me dry in the woods, I headed back to my trailer, with Six following close behind. I could see the regret in Six's face, but I didn't blame him one bit for what happened. *I* was the one that could've stopped it. No one else should bear that burden.

I took a cold shower, willingly scrubbing my skin raw and washing away any trace of Bram between my legs.

I needed this to end somehow, but I didn't want to risk getting kicked off the island. I didn't want to lose everything.

If succumbing to the things I didn't want meant I could keep the things I loved, I'd do it.

Over and over, again and again.

No matter how badly it hurt.

After pulling on my black, ripped jeans and a cropped grey t-shirt, Six and I headed to The Spider Tent. I told him about Bram being scared of getting replaced and not being good enough. Six couldn't give two shits about Bram—something I always admired about him—and didn't he care if he lost his timeslot, either. But if Bram goes down, then I go down too, and as much as he was praying for Bram's downfall, he didn't want to see that happen to me.

Through it all, nothing was in our hands. It was all up to Vark.

If Vark liked Dres more than us, we would have no choice but to switch.

And that would make Bram even more unbearable.

When we finally reached the tent, I could hear the faint sounds of shouting. There was a brief hint of a scuffle, and without hesitation, I ripped the tarp open and stepped through.

My eyes instantly locked onto Bram, who, for some reason, had hopped on stage, tackled Dres, and pinned him down on the stage below. Bram's fists were wrapped around the collar of Dres' black shirt as he yanked the cotton toward him.

I quickly ran down the aisle, passing the rows of empty seats, and made my way to the stage. Six followed.

"Bram, what the *fuck?*" I screamed, but Bram ignored me.

On his back, Dres lay on the stage as Bram straddled him. In a second, Bram lifted his right arm, keeping his fist clenched, and swung downwards.

Dres rolled his head and shoulders out of the way, letting Bram send a stiff punch into the solid floor.

"Fuck!" Bram cried out and immediately let go of Dres to cradle his hand. Finally reaching the platform, both Six and I hopped up. Six wrapped his lengthy arms around Bram, pulling him off Dres before he could try anything else.

"What the *hell* are you thinking?" I asked coldly, watching as Bram opened and closed his hand, flexing through a painful wince. Dres sat up and slowly inched backward, away from Bram's wrath, still oddly calm. Six let Bram go once Dres was far enough away.

"This *fucking asshole* set me on fire!" He motioned to Dres, who looked bored as he remained sitting on the stage. His knees were up and bent, and his arms were draped over top of them.

Bram raised his hips, allowing me to see the burn marks on the front of his jeans.

Black patches covered the surface of the denim, bunched together right near his crotch.

I looked to Dres right as his gaze found mine, and a quick raise of his eyebrows told me all I needed to know.

He did it on purpose.

He did it because of what he saw.

He did it because he saw *everything*.

"That's not magic, fucker. That's arson and attempted murder."

My eyes were locked onto Dres as Bram continued to rattle off a handful of threats. They all went in one ear and out the other as I continued to stare at him, swallowing a new trepidation in my throat.

I didn't see anything that just happened, but based on rehearsal yesterday, I didn't need to ask how he did it.

There was no reasonable explanation.

There was no way Bram offered himself as a volunteer, either. Dres doesn't even need an assistant, let alone volunteers.

Everything he does, he does alone.

"Damn it. I need to see a doctor."

My eyes snapped back to Bram. The back of his hand, specifically the space under his ring and pinky knuckles, was turning a deep shade of purple. You didn't need to be a doctor to know it was broken, fractured at the very least.

"Bram?" A voice echoed over the empty seats and reached the stage. The four of us turned to look. It was Vark.

Oh no.

"What's going on?" A meaty cough crawled out of his throat as he made his way down the rows and to the stage.

"Nothing," Bram answered, moving his hand out of sight.

"It's not nothing, Sir," Six interrupted, and Bram shot him a look. Six didn't care, nor did he hesitate. "He's injured."

"Injured?" Vark asked in confirmation, coming up to the platform. "Let me see."

Bram held his hand up gingerly as Vark got a good look at it under the spotlight.

"I just tripped and landed on it wrong. It's fine."

Vark sneered as his voice grew louder. *"Fine?* It's not fine. It's *broken."*

Bram tightened his jaw as the pain in his expression mixed with a fit of new, sudden anger.

"And don't tell me you fell. I'm not fuckin' stupid, Bram. I know what an injury from a punch looks like."

Vark eyed Bram, then me, then moved his eyes back to Bram.

"You two." He pointed to me and Bram. "My office. *Now."*

Oh, shit. *Shit.* Of course, I was getting roped into the consequences of Bram's mistakes. I should've expected it.

Sometimes, more often than not, I hated being Bram's assistant. No matter how good of a show we put on for the people, no one really knows what happens behind the scenes.

His actions always have consequences, and both affect *me*.

In the end, none of it plays in my favor.

Bram and I hopped off the stage and followed Vark. Glancing over my shoulder, I sent one final look to Dres. He was still sitting on the stage, in the same position, with his arms hanging over his knees. His eyes were already on me, and I felt a surge of physical heat run through me from just his stare alone.

It was different from the wave of ice that covered me when we first met, along with the chill he gave me less than an hour ago.

This was something more serious. This felt… intense.

But in that rush, Dres didn't look satisfied, angry, or anything in between. He simply looked as if he had nothing to do with this.

He looked indifferent.

And depending on what Vark had to say, I didn't think I could remain indifferent for much longer.

7

"Broken?" Bram asked in clarification as we sat in Vark's office. His hand was slowly and carefully being wrapped with a temporary bandage from one of the nurses on the island.

Vark slammed his drink down on his desk, making me jump in the lounge chair across from him. The ice clinked against the glass, and droplets of his alcohol splattered on the wood surface.

"Broken, you *fucking idiot*. What the hell were you thinking?" Vark leaned forward, staring unpleasantly at Bram.

"It was that asshole's fault! He *burned* me! He set me on *fire*, Vark. Who the fuck does that in a magic act?"

I looked down at my hands in my lap. As much as it sucked having my future in jeopardy this close to opening day, Bram was getting what he deserved.

Hopefully more.

"We are less than *two weeks* away from the big week. Two *fucking* weeks, and you go out and pull this shit?" Vark's face was beginning to turn red from the stress. "Un-*fucking*-believable."

"It's fine," Bram spoke in between yelling. "All I need is a couple of days off and some more bandages and I'll be fine."

Vark slammed the palm of his hand on the desk. "You can't even bend your fingers! How are you supposed to do half the things in your performance if you can't grab anything?"

"I'll push through it," Bram suggested.

"No," Vark pointed a finger at him. "I don't need people noticing an injury. They'll see you struggle once, and then that's all they'll think about for the rest of the show. They'll focus on you instead of the illusions."

Oh, God. This wasn't sounding good.

"I'm not about to race a horse with a broken ankle. I don't need your hand being the talk of the island. I need perfection."

I looked up at Vark, then stole a glance at Bram. His throat bobbed in a nervous swallow.

"You're out."

Those two words had an instant sting in my chest. Bram jumped to his feet and rambled off his objections while fear took over my entire body.

No. No. *No.*

I needed this. This was where I belonged. This was my home.

"You can't do that, Vark. We're too close," Bram pleaded.

My eyes jumped from Bram to Vark, Vark to Bram, hoping something would change in his decision.

But it didn't.

"Too bad. You're going to help with next week's deliveries and stock the tents whenever they need it. Plus, you don't deserve to be in the prime slot. Not after the shit you just pulled."

My eyes widened. Knowing how close Vark and Bram are, this conversation was surprising. I figured Bram would get a slap on the wrist, maybe a good scolding, maybe even some docked pay. Never did I expect us to get *demoted.*

Both of us.

Vark kept his voice steady. "You almost hurt my best act."

And now, those two words created another sting in my chest. *Best act.*

We were no longer the best.

Dres was.

It was then I knew this conversation would've happened, even *before* the punch occurred.

Bram was just the match that lit the flame.

Bram slowly sat back down in his seat, feeling the same devastation from those words that I did. His wrapped hand rested on the arm of the chair, and the nurse brought him a bag of ice to place over his swell.

The earth-shattering feeling of hearing we were no longer the best was something we shared; that was obvious. We worked hard to get where we were, and the fact that it was so easily taken from us hurt more than it should.

With a new compassionate side of me in bloom, I wanted to reach over and put my hand over Bram's. I wanted him to know that we were, in fact, a team, and the repercussions of the situation felt annihilating.

But before I could extend my hand to his, he spoke up.

"Vark." Bram's voice came out broken. "Come on. I worked so fucking hard for this. I *need* this."

He said *I.* Not *we.*

Suddenly, I no longer felt that compassion.

Right now, in this moment, he was only thinking about *himself.*

It was like I wasn't even in the room.

I blinked away any hopeful thoughts that he might have looked out for me. He never has, and he never will.

If I wanted to stay here, if I wanted to keep myself afloat, I had to take care of myself and no one else.

I cleared my throat, knowing this was my only chance to save myself.

"Let me join another act."

From the corner of my eye, I could see Bram's head snap in my direction, but I ignored it. I didn't care if he was pissed, annoyed, or betrayed.

He blew any chance of me caring about him at all.

"Actually, Willa," Vark leaned forward and clasped his hands together, "that's why you're here, too."

I could see Bram narrow his eyes from my peripherals.

"I have an idea for you."

I tried to keep my composure and remain still, even though Vark's words threw me off guard. I'd do anything to earn my stay and keep my life here. I'd work with Six, I'd work backstage, I'd even change the garbage cans if I had to. There was no way I was about to lose everything for Bram's careless actions.

Whatever it was, I'd do it.

Vark's eyes were glued to me as he took an extended moment to reconsider his decision. But as a grin slowly crept up onto his face, I knew the decision was already made.

"You're going to join Dresden's performance."

"Fuck no," Bram shouted, jumping up from his chair once again. The bag of ice from his hand fell to the floor. "Like hell she is. She's *my* assistant."

I winced at his possessive words. He wasn't trying to remain a team; he was just claiming me and keeping me out of spite. He wasn't scared of losing me; he was scared of losing everything he had.

Good.

"Not for the next three weeks, she's not," Vark confirmed, pushing power in his voice.

I chimed in. "Have you talked to Dres about this?"

Vark gave a half-shrug as he leaned back in his chair, pulling his drink with him. "I mentioned it."

I waited for him to continue. "...And?"

"And... he didn't seem too keen on the idea."

"See?" Bram said, still standing. "He doesn't even want her."

Ouch.

"Sit the fuck down, Bram. You have no room to speak right now."

With a groan, Bram obeyed. He picked up the ice and placed it back on his hand.

Vark continued, speaking to me and only me. "Just trust me, Willa. He wasn't open to the idea, but he wasn't completely shut out from it, either."

After furrowing my eyebrows, I blinked. "Why do you want me with him? He made it pretty clear he doesn't work with anyone. Plus, I'm more than capable of dancing with Six and his crew. I've done it before. Or, I can entertain the guests on the paths between acts."

Throughout the night, dancers and entertainers mingled with the guests intermittently when shows were between sets. They created a spark in the air with their ribbon lights, glittery makeup, and ability to entice the visitors into a euphoric trance. They were all part of what made the week so special. There was never a lull in the atmosphere nor a moment of stillness. I loved it all, and I always loved watching those entertainers.

Vark responded, "That can be a backup plan, sure. But for now, I want you to work with Dresden."

"As his assistant?" I asked in clarification.

Vark nodded.

The room was still and quiet as the new adjustments lingered in the air. Bram was furious; I could feel it, and Vark was optimistic; I could see it.

I, on the other hand, was more than hesitant.

"Why?" I asked, my voice a notch above a whisper.

"Because, Willa," Vark said, softening his voice as well, "you know how magic works. You have all the tricks up your sleeve already. You know the ins and outs, and you have a stage presence that is undeniable. You just have to do it all with a different person."

His words made me feel a bit lighter. He was right; I was used to it all—the lights, the sounds, the sleight of hand, the mirrors. I knew what I had to do and when. I had all the secrets.

Illusion

But doing it all with someone who doesn't need me, want me, and will barely talk to me is a different story.

"Plus, I need to know how he does his tricks. For the life of me, I can't figure it out. I'm counting on you to tell me how it's done."

I hustled out of that office faster than my feet could take me. I almost broke out in a sprint before I heard a booming voice carry across the stone path, reaching my back and sending a chill across the nape of my neck.

"Willa."

I stopped at the unnecessary shrill in his tone. *Damn it.*

"We need to talk."

I closed my eyes and dropped my shoulders. I knew this was going to happen, but I was hoping to let the air settle a bit.

I turned my body around, coming face-to-face with the one person I was hoping to avoid.

I quickly blurted out my thoughts. "I hope you know I had nothing to do with this."

Bram gave a half smirk, and for a split second, I felt bad for him.

"I know you didn't."

His hair was still pulled back in a bun, but now loose strands were falling around his face. He looked distraught and, dare I say, almost remorseful. This felt more like the Bram I knew at the beginning of my life on the island. There was a softer side to him that I'd experienced before, and anytime I could see it, I drank it in. Maybe he wasn't going to hold any of this against me.

After all, we were in this position because of *him*.

Maybe he felt bad and wanted to apologize. Maybe he regretted his actions and the impact they had on me.

I could feel my eyes widen with an enthusiastic sparkle.

"But I want to make something clear," he began, and my heartbeat sped up. "You better not make me look bad."

My hopeful expression fell instantly.

"Whether that be by making *him* look better than me, or by you looking like shit and embarrassing me just from being associated with me."

I jerked back, confusion striking my face. "So, you don't want me to succeed, but you don't want me to fail?"

"Exactly. Do what you have to do to make Vark happy, but don't you fucking dare be perfect. Not with *him*. You're only perfect with *me*."

God, the arrogance of this prick was unbelievable. He was making it so easy to hate him, and any sorrow I had for him completely disappeared in that moment.

"Bram, you're not making sense. *You're* the one that put me in this mess. This is because of *you*."

"No, this is all because of that stupid fucker. None of this would be happening if Vark didn't bring him here."

I didn't try to hide my obvious eye roll. Bram was refusing to take *any* accountability, all while acting childish at the same time. Typical.

"Whatever. Good luck with your new job," I scoffed, annoyance echoing in my words. I turned to leave, but Bram's hand grabbed my elbow before I could turn all the way around. I looked down at his fingertips digging into my flesh, his vice grip on me strong.

"I mean it, Willa," he said through a tight jaw. "You won't like me if I hear anything I don't want to hear."

I tried to yank my arm out of his grasp, but he tightened his hold and pulled me closer. "I already don't like you, asshole."

He chuckled. "Oh, I don't think that's the full truth. No matter how far down you have to dig, there will always be a part of you that will never stop wanting me. Remember the night after our very first show together? The way you rode my cock all night long, like the little *magic rabbit* you are?"

I forced down a swallow as he leaned in closer, whispering low.

"Remember screaming my name? Remember how sore you were the next morning, but already gearing up for round two? We spent that whole day fucking up until we had to perform again. God, you were so wet for me, and so *fucking tight* back then. So inexperienced, but everything came so naturally. *You* came so naturally." His body pressed against mine, and I could feel his solid erection along my hip.

My eyes darted to his, my gaze flaring with a new rage. "I was sixteen, Bram."

He licked his bottom lip. "What I would give for you to be sixteen again."

I pulled my arm again, and this time, I successfully got it away from his grip. My red curls bounced as I stumbled away from him, his stupid smile still painted on his face.

"Remember what I said, Willa," he called to me, the underlying threat more than clear.

I ignored him and walked down the path, making my way to the one person I *really* needed to talk to.

I stepped up to Lot 22 and knocked on the front door twice. Glancing from side to side, I focused on the fact that there was no one around, which wasn't too strange at this point. Everyone was frantically getting ready for the week, with only thirteen days left to prepare. Even though it sounded like enough time, it was sure to fly by.

It always did.

The thought startled me.

Less than two weeks, and I'm being thrown into a new act with a new magician.

Good thing I do well under pressure.

There was no answer, so I knocked again, this time tapping harder. Right after my hand hit the wood for the third time, the door swung open.

Dres stood there in a black sweatshirt and the same black jeans from earlier. His hair was a mess, his cheeks were a rosy pink, and he could barely squint one eye open at me.

"I—" Stumbling on my words, I tilted my head to the side. "Sorry, were you sleeping?"

His sleepy eyes stayed on mine as he blinked once, not bothering to try and wake himself up. He said nothing and only raised his eyebrows slightly.

When I knew he wasn't going to answer me, I shifted on his front step. "Uh, well. I'm not sure if you've talked to Vark at all… but…"

Dres leaned his forearm against the doorframe, keeping himself upright as he watched me talk. My gaze trailed up his arm and landed on the hand that dangled in the space between us. I wanted him to interrupt and tell me he already talked to Vark, to tell me he knew everything, and to tell me he was okay with the decision.

But he didn't.

He just blinked again.

I rested my hands on my hips as I continued, getting right to the point. "He wants me to join your show."

I expected an eye roll, a scoff, anything. But I got nothing.

He gave no reaction whatsoever.

"As your assistant."

Once again, no reaction.

I pressed. "Is that okay with you?"

Not that he had a choice, but I wanted to know his thoughts.

After a few more slow blinks, Dres finally gave me a piece of an answer through a lift of his shoulder.

He shrugged. That was his answer. *A shrug.*

I narrowed my eyes at him. "Do you care?" I asked with more venom in my words than intended, and not surprisingly, it didn't faze him in the slightest.

Moving his forearm off the doorframe, he brought his hand up to his dark hair and ran his fingers through it. Still no vocal answer.

I was growing irritated.

"Fine," I lifted my chin, brushing off any hope for his approval. "When do you want to practice?"

He gave another droll stare, this time accompanied by a sigh. "We're not going to."

I froze. *"What?"*

With the heel of his palm, he rubbed his eyes, and it was clear all he wanted to do was go back to sleep.

I pressed further. "What do you mean? I have no idea what your act is like. We need to rehearse."

"No, we don't."

My eyebrows practically reached my hairline in shock. "Are you out of your mind? You're going to force me to go into the big week completely *blind?* You're setting *both of us* up for failure."

I thought back to Bram's words and the threat that came with it. If Dres really won't practice with me, I know for a fact things won't go smoothly, and in turn, it will piss Bram off.

"Please," I begged, softening my face. "I know things might be weird for you, and you're used to being alone, but please, don't do this."

That's when Dres paused. He looked at me, *really looked,* and watched as I almost crumbled before him on his front steps. The fate of my life on this island rests in his hands and the magic show he creates.

His ice-blue eyes found mine, the irises glimmering in the impending twilight.

Illusion

He leaned forward an inch, slightly bending at the waist, as if he was telling me a secret.

"Have you done any archery illusions before?"

I narrowed my eyes. "Like… bow and arrow? Of course."

"Good," he replied. "Then we don't need to practice."

And with that, he closed the door, leaving me alone on his front step.

I stared at the slate grey color in front of me, confused and baffled and *bewildered* as to what just happened.

9

Restless sleep and cold showers were doing absolutely nothing to help ease my anxiety. The last time I talked to Dres was eleven days ago when he closed the door on me with only the subject of archery to hold onto. And since then, I haven't been able to shake the feeling that this was going to end badly.

So, I tried to fight my way into rehearsing. But every time I knocked on Dres' door, there was no answer.

Whenever I tried to catch him heading out of his trailer, I was left waiting on my front step with no sign of him.

Every time I tried to talk to Vark about it, he dismissed me, placing his total faith in Dres.

And, *technically*, me.

But I had no idea what we were doing. What *I* was doing.

I tried convincing Vark to let me do something else, but he wasn't having it. I even offered to work with Bram in his new job, which was helping Troy with whatever he needed. I would actually enjoy making cinnamon almonds, and it was a legitimate offer I could put my heart into.

But no. Vark didn't want that. He wanted me with Dres.

And just like Bram, whatever Vark wants, Vark gets.

So, sucking it up, I agreed. I agreed to walk into the week blind, despite every bone in my body screaming for me to jump ship.

But there was one last thing I wanted to try.

Heading over to Lot 22, I put on a brave face as I approached the door. It looked the same as the hundred other times I tried knocking on it, but for some reason, this time felt different.

I knew he was in there. I could feel it.

There was no way he was going to ignore me this time.

I knocked three times, my knuckles familiar with the soft pain from the grey wooden door. Stepping back, I shoved my hands in my back pockets, hoping for a greeting but expecting the inevitable ignore.

My hope was right.

The door gently and slowly creaked open, revealing a sliver of Dres. His eyes connected with mine, and I gave him an understanding glance along with a small smile.

"Hey," I spoke softly.

His only response was a tilt of his head.

"I'm not here about the show," I assured. "I promise."

Dres opened the door a bit more, showing off a grey t-shirt, a black zip-up sweatshirt, and black jeans.

"Do you have a minute?"

No answer, just his usual bored glare.

I hitched my thumb over my shoulder, motioning to the treeline behind me. "I want to show you something. It won't take long, I promise."

Dres' blank gaze turned to confusion as he furrowed his eyebrows. If he didn't want to go with me, fine. If he hated me, whatever.

This was going to be the last olive branch, the last stretch of my hand, the last offering I would give him.

Dres moved behind the door, leaving it open only a crack. I waited for something: a door slam, an eye roll, or a *"no"* if I was lucky.

But he surprised me. He put his shoes on and stepped out of his trailer, closing the door behind him.

He was agreeing to come with me.

Stepping away from his new home, he moved closer to me. I couldn't help but let a genuine smile spread across my lips at the fact that I was right.

I knew this time would be different.

Somehow, in some way, I just knew.

He noticed my smile as his eyes dropped down to my lips, studying the emotion I released out in the open.

But as quickly as he glanced down, he moved his eyes elsewhere.

And I took that as a cue to go.

"I want to show you something," I voiced, leaning into him slightly.

By his nature, he didn't respond.

But he did follow me as I began walking.

I took him up the trail in the opposite direction of the main grounds. We passed the large, wooded area, where there wasn't anything to see besides nature's creation. The leaves reflected a green hue, the tall trees cast brown shadows, and the combination of the two created a beautiful atmospheric relaxation.

It was quiet, it was peaceful. It was a nice break from the noise.

But we carried on without any words to one another, headed out of the woods, and found ourselves at the one place I wanted to show him.

Therapia Point.

The view was beautiful, and it took my breath away every time I came here. The skies were a perfect cerulean, with only hints of pure white clouds along the horizon. The water washed up to the shore with a bubbly white foam cresting along the edge, lapping up onto the dark rocks that made up the majority of the ground below. It was a perfect combination of blues, blacks, and whites, and it was a setting I've admired in my dreams hundreds of times.

Stepping out onto the rocks, I watched my placement, careful not to lose my footing. I could feel Dres behind me, and to my surprise, he stuck close to me.

I could've sworn I even felt his hand graze my back, ready to steady me if I needed it.

It didn't go unnoticed.

We found ourselves close to the point where the waves met the tip of the island.

I said nothing, and he said nothing.

The silence was comfortable. Even though I had a million thoughts running through my mind about the week ahead, I was able to quiet them with the serenity of the point.

It worked every time.

After a few minutes, I glanced over to Dres, who was still watching the waves ahead.

"This is Therapia Point," I explained. "It's not a secret, even though it seems like it is. Everyone here knows about it, but people only come here when they need water."

"Water?" he asked.

I nodded, then pointed to a tall cliff behind him. He turned and followed my gesture. "There's a waterfall. That's how we source our freshwater."

Dres nodded, soaking in this new information.

It was good to know, but I didn't bring him out here to tell him about the water on our island.

"When I first came here, I was so young and terrified of performing. I never had a *job* before, let alone been a performer in a magic act. It was brand new territory for me."

Dres didn't look at me, but I knew he was listening.

"On the day of my first show, a friend brought me out here. It was the first time I had ever seen the point, and I'm not sure what it was, but it instantly calmed something in me. It still does."

We both balanced on uneven rocks, watching the waves filter onto shore, the white spray mixing with the dark grit.

"Every year since then, I've been coming out here before every 'week.' But I also come here whenever I need to think. It puts me in the right headspace."

There was a quiet stillness between us, and I knew I had to say what I wanted to say.

"I'm not trying to guilt you into talking to me about our act tonight. It's too late for that, honestly. Whatever happens, happens. But I do want you to know that I can't fuck this up, and I can't let you fuck it up for me."

He ripped his eyes away from the ocean and glanced at me.

I swallowed, glimpsing briefly at the dark freckle under his right eye.

"This is my life, Dres. And it's going to be your life, too. Once you get a taste of this island, it's hard to think about letting it go."

Dres kept his gaze on me, absorbing every word I spoke.

"Don't let us fail."

With the ocean's waves crashing onto the rocks, snaking their liquified movements through the earth's crevices, Dres' jaw tightened in reluctance.

But then he said two words that almost calmed me as much as the view ahead of me.

"I won't."

Back at my trailer, I crossed my arms over my chest, the reality of the impending week hitting me hard.

About one thousand guests were flying to the island tonight. They were scheduled to arrive around six o'clock, and Dres and I were set to perform at ten o'clock. I looked at the time on my phone as I balanced a smoking cigarette between my fingers. Four PM.

Six hours until showtime.

Dres and I didn't talk on our way back from the point. When we reached the lots, we looked at each other, and a new understanding was balanced between us. *"See you soon,"* was spoken, and then we went our separate ways.

In the direction of the main grounds, I could hear the muffled hum from all the workers hustling in their respective tents. People were getting ready. I could smell the warm scent of freshly popped popcorn, Troy's potent cinnamon sugar mixture, apple cider and coffee, to name a few. Entertainers were dressed in vibrant colors with extravagant hair and makeup, and their props were ready to go.

Nothing compared to the rush of this week. Nothing.

As I sat on my front step, with my knees up toward my chest, Six hobbled by. He was on stilts as he called out to me, and I had to crane my neck to see his face.

"I can't *fucking wait* to see you work your magic, babe," he said to me, looking down with his arms stretched wide. "You're going to be absolutely amazing."

His words warmed me and forced a sincere grin to form on my lips. Of course, I'd obviously been nervous to step into this week, but Six never had any doubts about me. Or this.

And that eased things a bit.

"Thank you," I replied softly. "Don't let Link take all the shine this week, got it? Don't let his kneecaps faze you."

"Oh, hell no. This is *my* week."

I laughed and blew a kiss up to him. He pretended to grab it and stick it to his own lips, then flashed me a performative smile.

Then, with a soft nudge of his stilt against my leg, he wandered off toward the path, preparing for what was to come.

I exhaled. I had no other choice but to get ready.

My body was showered, tanned, and waxed. My hair was washed, dried, and curled. My clothes were clean, pressed, and tight. My makeup was applied, brushed, and blended.

Almost three hours later, there was nothing left to do but wait for showtime.

But there was no way I could do that alone.

Stepping out of my trailer, the brisk, chill air hit my skin. It wasn't terribly cold out, but it was enough to bring a jacket along. Slipping the forest green fabric on, I pulled it closed over my chest, leaving only my black tights and combat boots visible. I grabbed my carton of cigarettes from my jacket pocket, fished one out, and stuck it between my lips to light it. Along with the click of the lighter, I heard a voice behind me.

"You shouldn't do that."

I turned, the white stick releasing smoke only inches from my face. Dres walked closer to me, and the smoke caught in my lungs, forcing me to struggle out a cough.

Holy shit.

He had on boots similar to mine, his dark, faded jeans hugged his long legs, and his black sweatshirt covered a white cotton shirt that poked out from the neckline. His hair was smooth and carefully slicked back, with a few pieces free and hanging down over his forehead.

He didn't look like a magician. He looked like a normal guy, and he looked… *really good.*

Really, *really* good.

He approached me with his hands in his front pockets, looking like he had no care in the world.

Must be nice.

He motioned to the cigarette that was now between my fingers at my side, and I then realized *that's* what he was talking about.

"Do you want one?" I asked.

"No," he answered quickly. "Neither should you."

I squinted my eyes as I blew out a silent breath. Okay, okay. It was obvious he didn't like smoking, but he didn't have to be a dick about it.

I let his rudeness go and tried to feed off his thoughts. "I know," I admitted. "I've tried to quit."

As the last word left my lips, any hope I had of having an *actual* two-way conversation with him was crushed the moment I realized he wasn't stopping to talk to me. He kept walking as he let my answer roll off his shoulders. The only conversation he was making was in passing.

No. *No.*

This wasn't fair, not after the light yet significant moment we shared at the point. For the next seven days, we were together whether he liked it or not. I wasn't about to float through the week with only *"Hi"*s and *"Hello"*s and nothing else.

"Hey," I called after him, jogging to catch up with his stride. "Wait."

He didn't wait.

I quickly dropped the cigarette to the ground, crushed it, and continued to walk with him. Maybe that's why he doesn't want to talk to me. *Do I smell like smoke?*

I brushed the thought away. "Where are you going?" I asked with one hand still keeping my jacket closed.

He gave a shrug. *A shrug.* One more of those, and I'm going to send a spear right into that fucking shoulder.

No more questions. Questions only open the opportunity for him to either shut me out or piss me off.

"I'm going with you."

I caught the way his eyes gave me a side glance and used that as permission. Not that I needed it.

"Is that what you're wearing for the performance?" I asked, then immediately caught myself.

No more questions.

"You can't wear that for the show," I corrected my speech with a quick clear of my throat. "Wait until you see all the other performers. Everyone dresses up. They look amazing all the time."

"I'm wearing this," he replied, not bothering to look at me or take a second glance at his clothes.

I rolled my eyes. "We're not going to match."

"Do we need to?"

The corner of my glossy lips curled up in a grin. Finally, he asked *me* a question. "Yes."

We both approached the wooden fence. I hopped over first, careful not to snag my tights on any splintered pieces. The last thing I needed was another rip in my stage clothes. Dres followed suit, and our strides fell in line once again.

"Why?" he asked, referring to our clothes.

I turned my head to him and shot him a look. Was he being serious right now? "What do you mean? Dres, we are performers, and whether you want to be or not, we are now a team. Remember, you said you wouldn't let us fail. We have to do our part *and* look the part."

Dres kept walking but turned his head to look at me. It wasn't a side glance, and it wasn't a shrug. He looked into my eyes, searching them, trying to figure something out. I tried to blink away the sudden intimacy but failed.

"A performance," he echoed, not as a question but as a statement he could roll off his tongue.

I tilted my head and nodded as we approached the main grounds. People populated the paths, laughter was heard every way you turned, and not a single person walked by without a smile on their face. It was the beginning of something incredible.

Dres and I both stopped our steps as we studied the view before us.

Only hours ago, we were side by side at the point, watching the waves.

Now, we were side by side at the carnival, watching everything come together.

This was it.

This was *our time* to make magic.

There was a bit of a pause before he spoke again.

"I'm not like them," he said as he faced the new, dense crowd.

Thankfully, no one paid us any mind.

Yet.

Illusion

"I'm not a performer. My clothes don't matter. And if they do, the people are missing what they *really* should be watching."

10

Backstage, I shook out my hands. The jitters were real.

As much as I love doing this, sometimes my nerves overpower my confidence. My lungs squeeze a bit tighter, my hands grow a little slippery, and my heart jumps a beat too fast.

But in those nerves, I come alive.

I let the illusions take over and captivate the audience. The magic isn't in the trick itself; it's in the presentation. It's in the authentic love of the art, it's in the momentarily suspended belief, it's in the fleeting hypnotic trance.

Blink… and you'll miss it.

Behind the stage curtain, I paced back and forth in my black combat boots. My black, sheer tights trailed up my legs to my skin-tight black boy shorts that barely hid the curve of my ass. A snug, light grey spandex crop top covered the length of my arms and settled under my breasts, leaving only my stomach and neck exposed.

It was one of my favorite outfits, and it was perfect for night one.

Illusion

As I continued pacing, I scanned the area for Dres. He's been gone for almost twenty minutes now, and I was beginning to worry he bailed.

He wouldn't do that, would he?

Just as I began to silently curse under my breath, he came walking around the corner and headed to me. His sweatshirt was gone, leaving him in just a plain white t-shirt and the same faded jeans from earlier.

"We're on in two minutes," I whispered to him. The audience was already filling up, waiting for us to perform.

Dres gave a single nod as he kept his eyes out on the empty, bare stage, his presence eerily mild.

I sucked in a deep, nervous breath. "Okay, so you mentioned the bow and arrow illusion, right? Do you have the fishing line? I have the tube that can fit under my shorts and around my waist, I'll just need to get—"

"Don't." Dres cut me off, a look of aversion in his expression.

"Don't what?" I asked, staring at him.

He didn't answer, leaving me angry. *No more questions.*

"Okay," I continued, turning myself to get what we needed. "I'll go get the fishing line and the rubber arrows—"

"Stop."

With a gentle grasp on my wrist, *he stopped me. Dres stopped me.*

My eyes immediately dropped down to his hold. He had no strength in his grip whatsoever, but it was enough to catch and keep my attention.

"Stop with the stupid party trick shit."

His words were incredibly sobering as my eyes moved up to his, his gaze already piercing through me like a blade. My chest constricted at the first touch, the intense stare, and the lingering fact that we were about to go on stage.

And I didn't have a single thing up my sleeve.

"Dres," I whispered in complete fear. "We need it."

He didn't tear his eyes from mine. Not for a second.

"No, we don't."

I forced down a dry swallow as I began to sweat even more. Dres was really going to throw me on that stage without giving me an idea of what was happening. I was no better than an unsuspecting audience member.

The silence was deep between us as neither one of us looked away. His fingers rested on my wrist, my nervous heartbeat pulsing against his touch.

"You're on," a stagehand approached us quietly.

Dres dropped my arm. "Stay here. I'll let you know when I need you."

With that, he stepped out onto the warmly illuminated stage. Small string lights faded in and out along the sides in an intricate pattern, while one single spotlight stayed on him—and only him.

From the side, I watched as he performed, and my nerves slowly dwindled after not focusing on them. He did some of the same tricks from the other day, with the fire on the floor and on his arms. From this angle, I figured I would be able to see how he did it and find some hidden props that no one could see from the audience.

I was wrong.

With every motion, with every breath he took, I was still unable to place how he did any of it. My eyes tracked every movement, my attention focused on every trick, and I found myself holding my breath as I watched his performance.

The audience didn't let out the standard, boring "ooh" and "aah" like they usually did. No. They were gasping in shock, they were whispering words to each other, and they were completely entranced by him.

His magic was effortless. His illusions were seamless.

And I found myself in the exact same position that I was in when I watched him the other day.

I was oblivious to his tricks.

After a few minutes, Dres looked over his shoulder to me. With a tilt of his chin, he acknowledged me, and I took that as my cue to enter the stage. Slowly, I stepped out from the side curtain without a single hidden prop, nothing in my sleeves, and not a clue as to what I was getting myself into.

My nerves were back, and I was fucking terrified.

Dres extended his arm to me, palm up, reaching for me. The corner of his lips turned up in a subtle smirk, so subtle that my fear almost convinced me it wasn't real.

None of this was real. This wasn't happening.

As soon as I placed my hand in his, Dres pulled me closer to him. With a quick spin, he sent me in a twirl, and my body fell into the rhythm he was giving me. As soon as I faced him again, he pulled me flush against his chest and dipped me back, his other arm cradled against my back. My red curls draped down off my shoulders, my knees bent against his legs, and my hand was still clutched in his, all while everyone watched. It was the most emotion he has given me so far, and it completely caught me off guard.

He pulled me back up to him and let me go. My arms moved down to my sides as I faced the audience.

Dres circled me like a predator and his prey, but he never left me. His steps were close, and there was always one part of him in contact with me in each movement.

His arms grazed my sides, his shoulder brushed mine, and the back of his fingertips lifted ever so slightly to feel me.

It was his way of telling me he had this.

He knew what he was doing, even if I didn't.

Then, with his chest against my back, one hand reached up and grazed along my jaw. I turned my head toward him, playing into the intimate gesture. His face leaned down to me slightly, not too close, but close enough to create a new friction between us.

Then, for only me to hear, he whispered four words.

"Do you trust me?"

I immediately closed my eyes, feeding into the performance that was feeling extremely sensual.

I thought back to my tongue.

The four dollar bills.

The burn marks on Bram's jeans.

I matched his volume, answering quietly so the audience couldn't pick it up.

"No."

Dres let out a quiet laugh as his touch remained on my jaw. My eyes fluttered open at the sound.

It's like he approved of my answer. I told him what he wanted to hear.

He stepped away from my back but found my hand once again. Leading me to the back of the platform, he pressed me against the makeshift wall that hid the backstage area. It was a simple, black sheet of drywall, and it was only there for appearance reasons.

Dres ran a smooth hand over the majority of it, allowing the audience members to see that it was an actual wall. My eyes watched as he did it, and I could feel the nerves creep up again.

What was he doing?

He knocked a few times to insinuate it wasn't hollow. There were no doors, no hidden traps, nothing. It was something all magicians did in their acts, even though everyone knows those movements don't mean anything.

Everything's an illusion.

He held me by the shoulders and guided my back to the wall. I looked up at him, my eyes wide and pleading, unsure what he was doing, but I obeyed. I kept my back flush with the surface.

He walked out toward the front of the stage, stepping closer to the audience. Right below the front of the stage was a stagehand sitting in the shadows. He clearly wasn't meant to be a secret since Dres walked to him casually, but he wasn't noticeable until now. The stagehand held up a bow, two arrows, and a perfectly red apple.

Really? An apple? If I wasn't so nervous right now, I'd roll my eyes in front of everyone.

Dres gave the stagehand a silent *thank you* with a simple nod, then stood back up and faced me. His back was to the audience, which was a no-no. It didn't emit trust, only secrecy. He could be hiding *anything* regarding the trick. Even though it wasn't ideal for them, it was good for me. I could pick up on any secret facial expressions he wanted to give me to clue me in on what he was going to do.

But he didn't. His face was blank, relaxed, and carefree, as if we had practiced this hundreds of times before.

With the bow and two arrows in one hand, he held the apple in the other.

Then, with a quick smirk, he took a bite of the fruit. The crunch resounded in the quiet tent as everyone watched his effortless flow and waited for his next move.

While chewing, he walked up to me and placed the apple on my head, keeping eye contact with me the entire time. I could feel a drip of apple juice fall past my hair and onto my scalp.

He swallowed his bite. "Keep your hands down at your sides."

"Dres," I whispered for only him to hear, my eyes locked with his.

With the apple balanced on my head, he moved his free hand to his lips and held up his index finger in a hush.

He stepped backward to the front of the stage, never taking his sight off me.

He was toying with me, right?

He stopped at the edge. One more step back, and he would fall right off. I glanced down at his shoes, then back up to his eyes. I could feel the fear in my chest, gripping me from the inside out. My eyes began to instinctively water, but I pushed it all down.

I needed to focus. I needed to remain in the moment and not fall into my emotions. I needed to be professional.

But I couldn't help it. I felt like I was drowning in fear.

Dres dropped one arrow onto the floor next to him. The other arrow remained in his hand, along with the bow.

He held them both up and positioned them accordingly.

Some audience members got up from their seats and shifted to the side, trying to get a better look.

Dres held the bow to the side of his face as he balanced the arrow on the rest. Pulling one arm back and keeping his elbow straight, the string notched on the inside of his finger, and the tail of the arrow fit snugly against the cable.

My heart was in my throat, beating viciously against my skin. My shoulders were tight, my knees began to tremble, and my mouth felt dry.

But I forced myself to keep my eyes open.

Dres pressed his knuckles against his cheek as the arrow slid back. Both of his eyes remained open as his sight focused on the apple above me.

Then, with nothing but a release of his hooked finger, he let go.

The string bounced back with a fling as the arrow came at me.

But as quickly as it came, it vanished out of my vision, flying right above my head. It took everything in me to not duck at the sight of it speeding toward me.

The arrow vibrated only inches from the top of my head, and I felt more juice seep into my hair.

I glanced up. The arrow was through the apple, pinning it to the wall.

I let out the biggest fucking exhale as the audience cheered.

Okay. *Okay.* Thank God I was still alive. Half of me expected to take an arrow to the skull, and the other half didn't know what to expect. But now that I knew I was in one piece with no new holes in my body, I could breathe.

And as thankful as I was to know that I was still alive, I knew that wasn't magic.

That was skill. That was precision.

That wasn't a trick or an illusion. That wasn't a fishing line or a rubber arrow.

That had nothing to do with me.

I blinked as I tried to steady my pulse. Dres lowered the bow to his side, his stare still hot on me as an ease of satisfaction flashed through his face. The audience's applause faded as they awaited his next trick.

Dres bent down and picked up the other arrow. With a nod to me, he motioned for me to step back into place. I pressed my shoulders back to the surface with the apple still pinned to the wall above me.

My chest expanded with a deep inhale, causing my skin to stretch the tight, spandex crop top. He didn't have another apple, fruit, or *anything* to aim for. So, what was he doing?

Bringing the bow back up, he resumed the same position as before.

Bow outstretched.

Knuckles against his cheek.

The bend of his elbow parallel to the ground.

Arrow straight.

Eyes open.

Dres and I subconsciously inhaled, then exhaled, at the same time. Together.

The audience was dead silent as Dres let go.

The arrow came speeding at me, this time lower. Before I had a chance to dodge it, the pointed end hit me right in my left shoulder.

And for a half a second, I expected the arrow to collapse into itself. I expected it to maybe stick to me and my shirt, maybe bend at an angle where the audience couldn't see it. I expected something.

Not this.

That half second of expectancy completely disappeared when I saw the arrow lodged deep in my shoulder. Pain shot through the joint as I looked at the arrow that penetrated my body.

And I panicked.

The audience gasped as blood began to seep from the wound. My breathing turned quick and shallow as the new pain began to spread down my left arm. With my other hand, I covered my mouth and hid the cries that I so badly wanted to release.

Dres lowered his bow to the floor and slowly approached me. Hushed whispers continued to echo onto the stage, but all I could focus on was my shoulder and the pain that came with it.

A crimson circle spread in the fabric of my shirt as hundreds of thoughts ran through my head.

Would I be able to move my shoulder after this? Would I be able to perform after this? Did Dres do this on purpose so he wouldn't have to work with me anymore? Would I have to work with Bram for the rest of the week? Or, even worse, would Vark kick me off the island?

Dres stepped up to me, his eyes watching as my own began to fill with tears. Why would he do this?

He moved to my left side, allowing the audience to see everything happening. I refused to move my bad arm because I knew if I did, more pain would sharpen through the joint.

Dres led me toward the front of the stage as embarrassment heated my face. Everyone was staring at me and the blood that seeped from my wound.

But then Dres pressed one hand to the top of my shoulder while his other hand grabbed the wooden arrow.

Slowly, gently, and carefully, Dres pulled the arrow out from my shoulder. For some reason, it didn't hurt at all.

There was no pain. There was no ache. It was in my body one moment, then out the next, and I didn't feel a thing.

And that's what scared me the most.

The audience gasped at the sight of the arrow coming out of my shoulder. Dres held it up, showing everyone that it really *was* covered in my blood.

Not fake blood. Not corn syrup. *My blood.*

Tossing the bloody arrow to the floor, Dres moved his hand to the wound while the other was still placed on the top of my shoulder. He applied a bit of pressure, and a warmness spread over my skin.

My eyes remained on his hands as the pain that resided only moments ago was replaced with a foreign comfort.

Then, after a prolonged moment of silence, he moved his hands.

My shirt was ripped, but through that rip, I could see my skin underneath. There was no cut, no hole, no wound, and the only hint of blood was the dark liquid that remained saturated on my shirt.

If that wasn't there, it would've been as if nothing had ever happened.

Dres reached for me, his hand finding the edge of my jaw and brushing it lightly. I looked up into his eyes only to see a new smirk appear.

And the crowd erupted in applause.

11

Pulling on my cropped zip-up sweatshirt and jeans without first getting taken advantage of felt strange.

Incredibly amazing, but strange.

I half expected Bram to come and see me after the performance, to seek me out and make it a point to grope me, all because that's what he does. But while I anticipated him, he never found me. I wasn't even sure if he was at the show and had seen anything that just happened.

My mind was still spinning. I couldn't wrap my head around the fact that I was stabbed in the shoulder and then miraculously healed seconds later.

And I had *nothing* to do with it.

No sleight of hand. No mirrors. No fake arrows.

Nothing.

After everything that happened, Dres ushered me off the stage and did more enchanting tricks by himself. I waited until he was completely done with his set before changing into my street clothes, just in case he needed me again.

He didn't.

Illusion

He only needed me for the bow and arrow illusion, which was fine with me because my hands were shaking and I couldn't form a coherent thought afterward.

Once he was done, he walked off stage and passed me, not bothering to spare me a single glance.

Not that I was *trying* to get his attention, but he could have at least given me some sort of reassurance. Maybe even an explanation. After all, he *stabbed* me.

I got up and followed him.

"Hey," I called out to his back. "Thanks for the heads-up about, you know, shooting me with an arrow."

There was no one around, so I willingly spoke loud enough for him to hear me.

He ignored me and kept walking toward the back exit of the tent. His stride was quick, as if he had somewhere to be.

Or maybe something to avoid.

"A little warning would've been nice," I added.

Dres stopped suddenly, causing me to stop as well. He turned around to face me, his expression emotionless as pieces of his dark hair fell down over his forehead.

"Would you have let me use real arrows if I suggested it?"

His voice was calm. I paused.

"Would you have trusted me? Or would you have demanded me to use fake arrows?"

His tone wasn't harsh, and his words weren't laced with spite. He was simply asking a question, one we both already knew the answer to.

Of course, I wouldn't have trusted him. No one would've.

I reeled back, confused by his calmness and his expectations for me to feel the same.

"Are you fucking kidding me?" I asked, and his face matched my confusion.

"You think after talking to you *three* times in my entire life, all of which were *me* talking to *you* and *you not responding*, I'm suddenly going to trust you? Even after you refused to practice with me, or even just tell me your plans for the routine?"

Dres didn't reply, and I continued.

"You think your own assurance in yourself makes it okay to *stab me*? You *physically* hurt me, Dres. You made me bleed in front of everyone. And you couldn't even give me a heads-up because you thought I'd simply *look* at you and magically trust you."

I stood straight and held my stance. I was tired of being hurt.

Dres was proving himself to be just like Bram, except Bram at least *communicated* with me.

"You're all the same," I said through clenched teeth and miserable eyes. "All of you."

My voice cracked on the final statement, causing me to immediately close my mouth and straighten up.

I wasn't going to fall for this. Not again.

I'm done with being hurt. I'm done with being taken advantage of.

Dres glanced down to the ground, unable to meet my eyes anymore. I watched as he licked his bottom lip, preparing to say something, but then he didn't.

He turned and walked out of the tent.

No apologies, no explanations.

No reassurance, no consolation.

Just silence.

As he stepped out, Six stepped in. His smile was beaming, and his eyes were wide as he found me, his stilts nowhere to be seen.

"Holy shit, Willa. That was incredible!"

He clearly didn't hear the conversation that just took place, thank God.

I forced myself to channel my inner performer. Needing to gather my emotions and fake my sincerity, I returned the smile and scrunched my nose. "Yeah, it was, wasn't it?"

Illusion

I had no choice but to keep up the illusion. I had to be one step ahead of the crowd, other performers included, or else the entire premise of the show could fall apart.

No one can know that I didn't know.

Six wrapped his long arms around me and pulled me in for a hug. I laughed at his sudden embrace as he kissed the top of my head.

"I can't wait to see what else you guys have up your sleeve this week."

The voice in my head was loud.

Me too.

Six returned to his entertainment duties, leaving me to explore the grounds by myself. I found one of my favorite food tents, The Twisted Tent, and bought a perfect soft pretzel. It was fresh, warm, and had just the right amount of butter and salt. I got one every year, and my mouth watered every time I thought about it for the other fifty-one weeks of the year.

God, the lights and sounds of this place were incredible. The dancers were so eloquent, the activities were endless, and there was no shortage of excitement. For one week, my home turned into a perfect arena of adventure.

And when the sun set, things only got better as it all took an alluring turn. Guests gravitated toward the Onyx, Twyx, and Thryx Tents when they wanted an escape. The Onyx Tent emitted a haze of mysterious smoke, The Tywx Tent lit up with a neon red glow, and The Thryx tent was completely blacked out and soundproofed all the way around.

Vark wasn't too strict about performers exploring the tents and whatever else the island had to offer during the week, but he also expected us to remain professional in what we chose to do. Usually, I didn't do much besides eat, drink, and watch other performances. I liked to go back to my trailer and sleep after my act, especially after a whirlwind night like tonight. But there were nights when my adrenaline had no chance of slowing down, and I'd find myself chasing my own high in a similar sense to what Bram would do after our shows.

But instead of using someone else to satisfy my needs, I found safer outlets.

And after my unexplainable experience with Dres and the conversation that followed, I had pent-up energy I wanted to burn. There was no way I could keep my eyes closed with all the unknowns running through my head.

After finishing my pretzel, I stepped up to The Onyx Tent, opened the tarp, and made my way into the fog. There were couches, loveseats, and multiple cushioned bucket seats to sit in. Tables were scattered between all the furniture, creating a maze for people to find their way through.

And in that maze was an intense and completely opaque layer of white smoke.

I squinted my eyes as I made my way through the paths, struggling as I focused on a spot to sit. It was like a giant hotboxed tent, and I kind of admired the way the smoke shielded me from recognition from the guests.

I plopped down on an empty loveseat, instantly cradling into the soft comfort. Leaning forward, I grabbed a pre-rolled joint and a lighter and flicked on the flame. The end blazed in an orange hue as I took a deep inhale.

Smoke from other guests swirled around the room, enveloping me in an intoxicating haze. I closed my eyes at the serenity, basking in the high I was slowly but surely climbing. I felt my body and mind slip away into obscurity, and the soft stillness around me allowed me to relax for a few moments.

Or minutes.

I wasn't sure how long I was in my tranquility before someone nudged my shoulder, snapping me out of my trance. I lifted my head and opened my eyes.

"I think that guy is looking for you."

I turned to the voice, only to see someone I didn't know. He was leaning over the back of the loveseat with a joint between his fingers, and he motioned to a person standing at the front of the tent.

Dres.

His eyes were already on me as my stare found his. The smoke separated us, creating a clouded screen in my vision. I couldn't tell if he was angry, bored, annoyed, or all of the above.

All I knew was that he wasn't happy.

"He's the magician, right? The one that hit you with the arrow? That show was so fucking sick. How did you guys do that? I know a magician never reveals their secrets, but it looked so real…"

I ignored the guy and watched Dres. He approached me, still wearing the same outfit from the show, but now with the black sweatshirt pulled over his top half.

I made no moves to get up from my seat as he finally reached me.

His legs brushed against mine as he stood in front of me, and I couldn't help my heightened senses from reacting to his covered touch.

"Hey," the random guy said to Dres. "How did you guys—"

"Can you give us a minute, please?" I asked sincerely, and the random guy took the hint and backed off.

I sucked in another inhale of the joint, pinching it between my thumb and forefinger, then held it up to him. "Want a hit?"

He didn't answer. Instead, he crouched down with his arms resting over his knees, his eyes level with mine as I exhaled my hit to the side.

"I'll take that as a no," I spoke more to myself than to him.

Dres took a quick look around the room before glancing back to me, as if he were contemplating letting his thoughts come out into the open.

His voice was rich and deep. "It hinders me."

I furrowed my eyebrows. "What?"

He shook his head, refusing to explain any further. Before I could ask anything else—not that I *should be* asking anything—his low tone reached me again.

"What are you running from?"

My head cocked to the side instantly. "Excuse me?"

"You're constantly smoking. You're always anxious and tense. You're scared."

To him, it wasn't an observation. He spoke it as fact.

"The only time I've ever seen you relaxed was at the water."

"Therapia Point," I corrected, and he either dismissed me or ignored me.

I couldn't help but deflect at his words, words that made me instantly vulnerable and defenseless.

So, in turn, I put up any defenses I had.

"I could ask you the same thing," I spat back. "Why are you always running from me? Why do you avoid me?"

Remaining crouched in front of me with his gaze locked on mine, he didn't answer.

"Like it or not, we're a team, Dres." I placed the joint on the table beside me and leaned forward, keeping my palms on the soft cushion under me. "I know you didn't sign up for this, but you can't keep me in the dark forever. I refuse to step onto that stage blind again."

My soft, red curls fell over my shoulders and rested on my chest as my face neared his. I watched as he slowly took my words, inhaled them, and processed them.

Just like the smoke that lingered around us.

I just hoped that my outspoken thoughts broke through to him, giving him the same kind of high I chased.

Then suddenly, Dres dropped his knees to the floor, leaned closer to me, and grabbed my face with his hands. His thumbs rested under my jaw as his other fingers cradled the back of my head, forcing me to look up at him slightly. My hair fell back, and my eyes glistened through the haze in this new, personal position.

His voice was dark, cold, and just barely above a gritted whisper. "If we are a team—*like you claim we are*—then you're going to have to trust me."

Trust.

I replayed the word in my head over and over.

Trust. Trust. Trust.

I decided to take a leap of faith and ask him something in hopes that he would actually give me an answer. Because if he wants my trust, he'll have to meet me halfway.

"Did you aim for my shoulder?"

He didn't hesitate. "Yes."

"Why?"

His eyes volleyed back and forth between mine, as if he was searching for the right words in my gaze.

"Why didn't you tell me you were going to *stab me?*" My words were pierced as I punctuated the last two words through the clenched jaw he held.

Even though I knew he had one, he didn't give me an answer, which I should've known was going to happen.

Instead, he changed the subject.

"You need to cut this shit out," he began, his tone clipped as he matched my stern expression. "Stop smoking. Stay sharp. Keep your eyes open. Stop running. Cut the cigarettes, too. That shit isn't doing you any favors. If anything, it's making everything worse."

We both paused as a fresh, raw passion bounced between us. He was right; smoking was my escape. I used it as a crutch when I was stressed, when I needed some sort of release, and it usually only masked my feelings of dread for a minute or two. Then, I was right back where I started.

My heart was beating steadily against my chest as I awaited his next move.

His ice-blue eyes held mine, and for a moment, I thought he was going to kiss me. With the tension between us, I almost *wanted* him to kiss me, which was a completely foreign feeling.

Why did I want him to kiss me?

Was I just searching for the forced intimacy I knew so well?

Did I expect it from him just because I was his assistant?

I tuned out all the possibilities swirling around my head. For once, I wanted to lead *myself* with my *own* emotions, not with others' expectations. I *wanted* that authentic connection to seal its fate in our embrace, leaving the prior events of the night behind us.

But as I waited, the kiss never came.

I knew he had something else up his sleeve. He always did.

"From here on out, the only smoke you're going to take is mine."

One of his thumbs moved to my chin, then to my bottom lip. He pulled it down gently, parting my lips and exposing the smallest gap in my mouth. His eyes flared with a desire so subtle yet incredibly readable, and I found myself basking in the heat. My entire body warmed at his intensity, and I suddenly felt a wave of need rush through my core.

Dres leaned down and opened his mouth, just barely, and my hooded gaze moved to it.

A pure, white fog escaped past his lips as he exhaled an unknown smoke. On instinct, I inhaled, absorbing everything he was giving me, and I couldn't help but close my eyes in a trance.

To everyone else in the tent, it looked like an intimate, common smoke exchange, but it wasn't.

This was more.

The curled smoke that slid down my throat and filled my lungs felt like clean, cold ice. My body erupted in chills, my insides tingled, and I felt like I was breathing in the cleanest, most pristine air. The feeling was euphoric, and it was giving me a high that no other drug could come close to.

It felt addicting without the addiction.

It felt captivating without the captivity.

It fulfilled me without weighing me down.

And as he finished his exhale and closed his lips, I entered a blissful state of delirium that I had never felt before.

And I knew, in that moment, whatever he was giving me was undoubtedly tying me to him.

12

Night two.

The audience was packed once again, but now more people were lining up along the tent walls. There were no seats left, so those who came to watch had to stand. It was only night two, and word was already spreading about our show.

Not surprising, since it happens every year. Sometimes, people don't know there's a magic show right away, and by the end of the week, we are always sold out.

But this was all happening ahead of schedule. Word must've spread *fast*.

I stood alone behind the curtain as the lights dimmed. That was our cue to go, and I still had no idea what I was in for. Dres wasn't around for me to ask.

Last night, after he gave me his mysterious vapor, he simply up and left.

Of course, everything inside of me was *screaming* to find out more about his mysterious smoke. I had no idea where it came from. Was there a hidden mint in his mouth that created a heavy vapor? Was there something up his hoodie sleeve?

Was there an explanation for *any of this?*

But before I could ask, he left. There were no more words exchanged. No more explanations. No more reasoning.

Just the gentle push of his hand under my chin, closing my lips, keeping the smoke contained inside of me.

It wasn't long before I left, too.

I looked down at my light blue, square-neck body suit and dark spandex boy shorts and attempted to smooth out any wrinkles. I checked my high ponytail, making sure the red curls cascaded down the backs of my shoulders flawlessly. I could only stall for so long before we would have to postpone the show.

Crowds don't like it when acts are late. *I* don't like being late.

Just as I was about to turn around and abandon ship, Dres walked up behind me, heading to the stage. As he brushed past me, his eyes connected with mine, and his look said it all.

He was ready. He knew I was hesitant.

But he wasn't stopping. He wasn't waiting for me.

We were doing this, whether I was ready or not.

I swallowed the lingering nerves as I watched him step out on stage, not saying a word to me but not breaking eye contact, either.

His attention was on *me,* and probably the things he was about to do *to me,* rather than impressing the crowd.

And I wasn't sure if I liked that or not.

He was wearing a different pair of faded, lightly scuffed jeans but the same plain white t-shirt. Or maybe it was a different one. How many white t-shirts did this guy have?

He wowed the audience with more tricks that were simple to the eye but not to the mind. Everyone could clearly see what he was doing, but their minds could not process *how* he was doing it. And from the side stage, with an unobstructed view, I couldn't figure it out either.

He was a puzzle I couldn't solve.

After his warm-up tricks, he extended his arm to me and brought me out on stage. My black combat boots barely made a noise as I followed his lead across the stage. While he was bringing me out, a stagehand brought out a barrel to the middle of the stage.

I looked to the Dres, then the barrel, then back to Dres.

I knew exactly what this was and where it was going, and I didn't like it one bit.

Bram and I did this trick a few years ago. A metal barrel was held up high, supported by hollow steel beams, and completely filled with water. I had to climb up to it, get in, and kneel down while a steel lid was placed over my head. The hollow beams discreetly sucked out the water, and I would then crawl into a second empty barrel. Then, the previous barrel would refill with water, giving the illusion that I would've been soaked, maybe even dead from drowning, but in reality, I was dry and hiding in the second barrel.

It was my least favorite trick, and that's why we never did it again.

With the lid over me and the possibility that the water might not drain, the illusion made me feel immediately claustrophobic and filled me with anxiety.

Plus, all in all, it was boring.

So, stepping out on stage to see this completely shocked me.

Instead of a metal barrel, it was clear.

Instead of it being held up with hollow pipes, it was on the floor.

Instead of a lid with an emergency breathing escape, there was simply a clear, flat cover.

There was no way to hide. There was no escape plan. There was no illusion.

Dres was trying to kill me.

"No," I whispered to him in fear, barely moving my lips so the audience couldn't see. My heart jolted at the thought of stepping in there.

All Dres did was stare at me, his blue eyes icing my skin, giving me a chill right here, in front of everyone.

Illusion

Still holding my hand, he pulled me closer. I took one step toward him, then another, until our chests were almost touching. One deep breath and my breasts would brush against his shirt.

"Do you trust me?" he hushed, moving the back of his hand up to gently slide against my jaw.

Trust. Trust. Trust. Trust.

"You're going to have to trust me."

I wanted to. I wanted to give him everything. All of me. Put everything in his hands.

But I couldn't.

Emotions came crawling up and out of my skin, finding their way to the surface of my outward mentality.

"I can't," I pushed out, my voice so quiet I wasn't sure if he heard me.

But with the audience so still, so silent, he blinked away a flash of disappointment, and I knew he heard me.

Turning his back to the audience, he never let go of my hand as he led me to the water tank. I was secretly hoping to find some sort of trap door, a tube for air, anything. But there was nothing.

It was a clear barrel of water on the floor. Nothing less. Nothing more.

Dres stepped around the left side while I made my way around the right, our hands remaining connected over the top. When we both reached the backside, he gave me one final look.

One that screamed trust. Confidence. Assurance.

Everything in my gut was telling me to place that trust in him, while everything in my mind was telling me this was wrong.

But I was on stage with hundreds of people watching.

There was no backing out now.

Letting go of Dres' hand, I placed both of my palms on the edge of the barrel. Dres wrapped his arms—strong arms, to my surprise—around my thighs and lifted me. I turned my body and sat on the edge, resting my weight along the rim, and Dres let me go once I had my balance.

Trust.

It wasn't fear that was giving me goosebumps on my bare arms.

It was his stare.

Trust. Trust. Trust.

And with one last inhale, I swung my legs over the water and dropped myself in.

I was completely submerged.

My chest constricted at the change in pressure. I blinked through the water, trying to gain focus, but all I could see was a light blur of the stage lights in front of me.

My red hair floated in the liquid around me as I began to tread the still waters, trying to keep myself from floating to the top. My boots were doing a decent job at weighing me down slightly, but I couldn't help but think I should've taken them off. They were clunky and annoying in this barrel.

I could feel an added pressure as Dres placed the lid on the barrel, and that's when I panicked.

Suddenly, reality set in.

I was in a pool of water with no way out and only seconds of air left in my lungs. Bubbles escaped my mouth as Dres leaned down on the other side of the plastic, watching me.

He put his hand flat on the barrel, and I looked at it.

My lungs were tightening, and I was fighting the urge to inhale.

But in that fight, I placed my hand with his, trying to gain strength through the plastic.

But there was nothing, and my fear exceeded my desire to keep my composure.

My hand clenched into a fist as I banged on the barrel, but the water's resistance prevented me from making any sound other than a light thud. I tried again, and nothing.

I opened my mouth to scream, only to let in a rush of water. My body immediately swallowed the influx of water, and my reaction was to cough.

Which led to another inhale. And another.

My eyes began to burn as I looked for Dres. He was still watching me with a look of concentration, as if he was studying me intensely.

I wasn't sure if that made me feel better or worse because I mostly wanted him to do *something*.

Help, I mouthed through the water, but it just looked like a scream.

I was going to die.

My vision began to fade into a dark cloud as my body weakened. I wanted to fight; I wanted to kick the lid off this and climb out, but my strength was wearing thin.

This was going to be my demise.

And as fast as it all started, it ended.

Next thing I knew, I was lying on the stage floor. I opened my eyes and inhaled as the bright, warm light above blinded me. Oxygen flooded my lungs, which felt surprisingly light. My breathing was normal, my head was clear, and my heartbeat was steady.

"Do you trust me?"

My mind instantly flashed back to last night with the arrow, and minutes ago in the water. I wanted to turn my head to the voice I've come to know, but I didn't have the energy. Dres leaned into my line of sight, blocking the light as it surrounded his head like a halo. His shirt was soaking wet, and I assumed it was from lifting me out of the barrel. He panted slightly as he remained over my body, dripping onto my already-soaked skin. To my own surprise, I didn't feel any pain, at least not in that moment. All I felt was his touch, his comfort, his safety.

A few seconds felt like hours as his eyes remained locked onto mine, waiting for an answer, as the silence from the invested audience echoed in the tented walls around us.

I tried to speak, urging myself to answer his question, but nothing came out.

His hand lifted under my chin, slowly adding pressure, beckoning me to sit up.

So I did.

I followed his touch as he led me forward, and I easily found the ability to understand him. I made my way to a sitting position, and then we both stood to our feet, all while Dres had his hand under my chin and his gaze locked onto mine.

Trust.

My answer was in the urge to follow.

The pressure to pursue.

The need to comply.

My body no longer felt weak from the water. My muscles were no longer tight from trying to chase the need to survive.

It was as if it never happened.

The crowd erupted in a loud cheer, standing to their feet in complete revolution. They were clapping, whistling, and hollering, all for us and whatever happened while I was out.

I turned to look at the audience and smiled. It was a genuine, yet confused, smile.

Then I looked back to Dres, who never once looked out to the audience.

He was only watching me.

13

I was wringing my soaked, red hair in a grey towel as Dres walked off stage. Six had just sent me another congratulations in passing but had to leave to get back to work before we could talk any more.

And, once again, Dres didn't bother to look at me before heading toward the back exit.

"Dres," I shouted to him, still squeezing the excess water out of my hair.

He continued to walk away as if he didn't hear me.

"*Dres,* would you just *listen to me?*"

Finally, he stopped at the edge of the tent, almost ready to walk out.

"You say all this stuff about *trust* and *teamwork* or *whatever,* but you never fucking *act* like we're a team." I could feel my blood pressure rising along with the volume of my voice. He turned to face me as I continued. "Don't expect me to trust you if you won't even talk to me."

His jaw hardened, and I realized that small look of anger was the most emotion he'd shown me yet. He took a step back to me, and then another, before stopping. Returning the steps, I moved closer, needing to get *whatever this was* out in the open.

His eyes peered down to mine, and I stared up at him. We were right back in the same position as we were on stage, but this time, no one was watching.

"What happened?" I asked with brisk anxiousness in my tone.

I wanted answers. I *needed* answers.

How did I go from drowning in a barrel to perfectly fine on the floor of the stage?

How did I feel so *safe* with him without knowing how I got to that safety?

My hand moved up to his forearm, grasping it gently. His skin was warm, *so warm,* as if flames had just danced on his skin moments ago.

My eyes moved down to his lips as I watched the full, round, natural pout he gave by simply existing. I could feel the electric current between us, pulling us together, magnetizing us. We had a harmony together that I didn't have with anyone else. Our moves worked together, our flow streamed together, and our souls danced together.

With everyone watching, we were *together.*

He knew it. I knew it.

But he wouldn't stop to admit it.

And as I was silently hoping for him to act on his emotion, he turned around and walked right out.

I groaned. That's it. Fuck this.

At that moment, I vowed to go to Vark's office first thing in the morning and switch jobs. I don't care if it's the start of the week. I don't care if I have to work a ticket booth or change garbage cans. At least it gets me away from the one person who clearly doesn't want anything to do with me.

With a bottle of water between my feet and a slight breeze in my hair, I rested my book in my lap as I turned the page. The weather was perfect, so I came outside to sit on my front steps and read for a bit before I needed to get ready for the third show of the week.

A voice snapped my focus away from my book.

"Willa."

I momentarily refused to look up as I swallowed an annoyed cry and scrunched my nose. I didn't want to do this. Not now.

Footsteps scuffed up to me, and I finally looked up to face the person standing in front of me. "Hey, Bram."

He gave me a quick nod of his chin as his eyes raked over my body, an action from him that I knew too well.

"You guys were good last night."

I hesitated. "You watched it?"

Bram nodded as he gently rubbed his neck with the white cast his hand was in.

I closed my book, letting my curiosity get the better of me. "What else did you think?"

Bram gave an effortless shrug. "I just told you, Willa. You guys were good."

There was an awkward pause. I know he didn't run all the way over here to tell me we were good.

"But… you and I are better."

There it is.

He grabbed a carton of cigarettes from his pocket and held it out to me as an offering.

I shook my head. "I'm trying to quit."

He stilled briefly before popping one out for himself and lighting it. He inhaled, then exhaled, all while I watched and suppressed my cravings for it.

"The only smoke you're going to take is mine."

I blinked away the intimate memory.

"You know," he continued through his exhale, "we just work better together."

He has to be out of his mind to think that's true. Yes, we work well together, but what we have doesn't compare to the mountain of chemistry Dres and I have together. And that's a fact Bram will have to accept, whether he likes it or not.

"Tell me how he does it," Bram quickly spit out, as if he needed to say it before he changed his mind.

"Does what?"

"Everything," he said, taking another inhale. "He's gotta have some sort of setup, right? I tried to figure it out, but he made it hard to catch everything. Plus, your acting was great. You looked like you actually drowned up there."

Drowned?

"Excuse me?" I nearly choked on my words as I furrowed my eyebrows, unable to help the shock that rang through my voice.

"Yeah. Adding an audience member to come help you was a nice touch."

I swallowed a new lump in my throat. After the show, I didn't talk to anyone besides the brief, one-sided conversation with Dres. I went home and went right to sleep. I had no idea what Bram was talking about, and I wasn't about to let him in on that. I needed to keep my composure and act like it was nothing more than an illusion.

I sighed out my praise. "Dres really knows what he's doing up there, that's for sure."

Bram studied me, narrowing his eyes by only a fraction. "Yeah. He does." He dropped his cigarette and stomped it out with his boot. "But you're still with *me*, right, Willa?"

He took a step toward me, and I leaned back.

"Yeah, Bram. Of course."

He squatted down to my level and looked me straight in the eye.

"Good. Because this is only temporary."

"Obviously," I said, hiding any dread that was trying to peek up. I grabbed my water and book and stood up, trying to put an end to this conversation before it turned into something it shouldn't.

"Hey, what do you say we head inside? Maybe we can have a drink or two?" Bram stood with me and nodded to my front door, his eyes still piercing through me with fervor. "I have about another hour before I have to head back."

I shook my head. "Bram, I need to get ready. Can we hang out some other time?"

Bram shook his head, knowing I was full of shit. It was only noon. I had plenty of time, but I'd say anything to push him away, time and time again.

"Nah, I think now's a perfect time."

God, here he was, chasing that adrenaline again. But this time, it wasn't his high; it was his fear. He was scared of losing me to Dres based on our sudden success, so he was making sure he had me in any way possible.

Part of me would prefer him to do this after one of our shows instead of at random times like this, so at least I can expect it and mentally prepare for it in time.

My back hit my front door as Bram stepped up to meet me. He pushed his hips into mine, and it took all my energy to not groan in disgust in his face. Reaching past me, Bram grabbed the doorknob and pushed the door open, forcing me to stumble back into my trailer.

I wasn't scared of Bram. Not in the slightest. But when he got in these moods, I couldn't help but experience a wave of dread wash over me.

Because I knew what was coming.

"Magic rabbit," he cooed as he followed me into the trailer. The front door fell closed but didn't latch completely. Reaching down, he grabbed my book from my hands. He looked at the glowing streetlight on the cover and scrunched his face.

"Since when do you read this shit?" He threw the book on my coffee table. "Looks boring as hell."

I wanted to correct him and tell him I've always liked reading; he just never noticed. Plus, since I was trying to quit smoking, I needed to busy my hands and mind with something else.

But he didn't care. Obviously.

"Bram, I—"

Before I could say another word, he grabbed my arms and flung me down on my couch, sending my water bottle sliding across the hardwood floor. Even though my body hit the plush cushions, cradling me in softness, it was still jarring to be tossed like that. I leaned up on my hands, ready to push back if needed.

"*Willa,*" he tsked. "Willa, Willa, Willa…"

Grabbing the bottom hem of his shirt, he pulled it over his head and tossed it aside.

"You're not very convincing."

I cinched my eyebrows. "What?"

He approached me, his good hand fumbling with his belt buckle as he did so.

"You say you're with me, but I see it written all over your face, baby." He pushed his belt out of the way and undid the button of his jeans. "You're not. You're with *him.*"

"Bram," I scoffed. "Stop. I've performed with him twice. I've performed with you for *years*. Don't make this into something it's not."

My words did no convincing whatsoever because in seconds, his pants were down, and his hard dick bounded free. My eyes remained focused on Bram's face as he stood before me like a man wanting to take complete control.

I could feel a rage brewing in the hollows of my being.

"You're with me?" he asked in confirmation. "Fine. Then prove it."

Oh, God.

I froze, my gaze still locked on his cruel, cold eyes.

"Fucking prove it," he barked. "Suck, Willa."

His good hand moved down to the base of his cock as he grasped it firmly. He slowly slid his grip up, adding pressure until he got to the tip, releasing a small drop of pre-cum on the swollen head.

"Lick it off," he commanded, and my heart broke a little bit.

I hated this.

I hated him.

I hated *myself* for somehow falling into this position.

Again.

I could feel the beginning of a tear rising to my bottom eyelid. To keep it from falling, I closed my eyes, hoping the liquid would settle under my skin and stay there.

And, if I didn't have to see what I was doing, I could block it out easier. I could picture myself somewhere else, doing literally *anything* else, as long as I wasn't here, doing this.

I opened my mouth and wrapped a hand around Bram's length just as the stray tear escaped past my eye and fell.

Then, the front door to my trailer burst open, hitting the wall behind it and making everything in the place rattle.

Bram and I both turned our heads to look.

Dres stood in the doorway with his short, dark hair mussed and unsettled, his black sweatshirt stretching along the span of his chest, and his pulse almost exploding out of his neck.

Holy shit. He was *furious*.

His skin was red and heated, and his eyes were almost black as he scanned the compromising positions we were in. His eyes skipped right over Bram and found mine, and I could see his gaze trace the tear that fell down my cheek only seconds ago.

Bram made no moves to cover himself and his naked ass. "Get the fuck outta here."

Before he could even finish the sentence, Dres ran up to Bram, grabbed him by the throat, and threw him down onto the coffee table. I hopped back onto the couch, pulling my legs up and away from the brawl. Dres hovered over Bram's body as he remained on the table, and Bram barked out the same command with a new quiver in his voice.

"I said *get the fuck*—"

Bram's yell was silenced by Dres' fist on the side of his mouth. Bram's bottom lip instantly split open, and a small line of blood rested on the surface.

"What the fu—"

Another punch silenced him, this time landing on the side of his nose. Bram's head snapped to the side, and another drop of blood pooled at the bottom of his nostril. A new fury overtook him as he scrambled to get up, but Dres wasn't having it.

With unrelenting strength, Dres placed a hand on Bram's shoulder to keep him from fighting back. And with one quick motion, he used his other hand to smash Bram's head back on the table, creating a loud cracking sound in the walls of my trailer.

Oh my God. He was going to kill him.

"Dres," I screamed, but he didn't pay me any attention.

Raising his fist, Dres sent another punch to Bram's eye. At this point, Bram was so dazed from the blows that he was no longer fighting back. He simply lay on my table with his jeans around his knees and a groan in his throat.

Getting up from the couch, I pulled Dres' arms away. "Dres, *stop it.*"

I felt slight resistance from Dres, but once he realized I was the one pulling him away, he relaxed his fight. A pathetic moan escaped Bram's throat as he rolled off the coffee table and landed on the floor. Droplets of blood dripped onto the hardwood as he slowly gained the strength to sit back on his heels. The silence was heavy in the trailer as Bram gingerly grabbed his shirt, put it on, and pulled up his jeans. Dres' breathing remained heavy in rage next to me as we watched him get situated.

Bram stood to his feet and turned to the door, but only after trying to get the final word in.

"You better watch your fucking step," he said, pointing to Dres.

And that made Dres snap instantly.

In a split second, Dres was back at Bram's throat, grabbing him and thrusting him against the wall next to the front door. Dres easily had a few inches towering over Bram, along with an impressive grip strength on his neck.

Despite the sudden reaction, Dres' voice remained eerily calm. "Touch her again, and I'll break the other side of your face. And your other hand, too."

Bram grit his teeth as his face reddened.

"As a matter of fact, if you even *breathe* near her, I'll set you on fire again. And this time, I'll make sure the flames never die."

My heart dropped to the pit of my stomach at his words. He was defending me, guarding me, protecting me.

Even though almost all of our conversations have been one-sided, he was here, in my trailer, fighting for me.

Something Bram never cared to do.

"So you *did* set me on fire on purpose," Bram shouted. *"I fucking knew it."*

"Never said I didn't."

A silent, sharp inhale filtered through my lungs as the two men stared at each other, their face-off angry and deliberate.

It was only a matter of seconds before Bram's gaze flickered to me briefly before pushing Dres' arms away. He knew he had no chance against Dres, considering his left eye was swollen and he only had one good hand remaining. He said nothing and didn't look back before heading out the door.

The quiet was deafening as it was now just Dres and me. He was rooted to the spot with his back angled to me. I couldn't see his expression, if he even had one at all.

What was I supposed to say?

Sorry?

Thank you?

Everything felt so generic and impersonal. I had nothing to be sorry for, and I felt like thanking him made me seem weak. Not that I wasn't grateful for what he just did, but I also didn't think of myself as a girl who needed saving.

And, for some reason, I knew he felt the same way.

I remained standing by the couch as Dres slowly turned to me. He ran a hand through his messy hair, and I took a second to admire the way it fell perfectly along the top of his head.

But upon watching him in the act, I saw the blood dripping from his freshly cut knuckles, and I was thrust right back into the unfiltered moment.

He did this for me.

My lips parted as I tried to speak, but no words came to the surface. There was no expression to match my emotion, and I couldn't figure out how to maneuver through these feelings.

But it didn't matter because when I looked into his eyes, I knew he didn't want to talk about it.

His stare was knowing, his jaw was set, and his shoulders rolled back in an uncomfortable adjustment.

He glanced down to my coffee table, first looking at the scattered blood, then glimpsing at the streetlight on the book cover that sat on the wooden surface.

"When you finish that, let me know if it's any good."

And then he walked out the door, shutting it gently behind him.

14

That night came and went without issue, except for the fact that Dres didn't use me in his performance. I stood on the side of the stage, waiting for a cue that never came. My hair was done perfectly, my makeup sparkled under the lights, and my clothes were slimming and revealing. I looked show-ready, but I guess Dres thought otherwise.

Even without me there, he performed flawlessly. It was obvious that he didn't need me, he *never* needed me, and I couldn't help but feel a little jealous that I wasn't out there with him, enjoying the magic he loved.

Because it was the magic that I loved, too.

Once he was done, the audience roared in applause, just as they had done the other nights as well. He casually walked off stage to me, watching me as I beamed a smile at him. He returned a small grin and gently grasped my elbow as he shifted his way by me.

But now, I wasn't hurt that he wasn't giving me the attention I used to crave. I looked at him with a new sense of pride, a sudden appreciation for his art, and an understanding that trust takes time.

"Do you trust me?"

Illusion

I watched him pull on his trademark black sweatshirt as I thought about the one question he was constantly asking me. And based on the events with Bram earlier, along with the knowing fact that Dres never lets me down on that stage, I began to feel a new wave of confidence blossoming from the inside out.

"Dres," I voiced, barely able to raise the sound loud enough for him to hear.

But he did.

He paused and turned to look at me, his blue eyes glinting in the twinkling fairy lights, his hands halfway down his torso as he pulled the cotton of his sweatshirt down.

I gave him another half-smile, tilting my head in the process. "You're incredible out there."

Dres looked down at his clothes as he finished getting dressed, and all I got was one simple word. "Thanks."

And with the one simple word, Dres left the tent. I had no desire to follow him or get any answers. I just stood there with a realization that even though he didn't need me, and I didn't need him, we were still a team.

Night four.

Dres didn't need me tonight, either.

I'd be lying if I said I wasn't slightly disappointed. Dres performs with such authenticity, charm, and enchantment, causing a big part of me to want to be involved. When he was done with his show, he turned to walk off stage, and I couldn't help but exhale a disappointed breath.

I kept my eyes on the floor as he passed me. And even though I could feel his arm intentionally brush against mine, I couldn't bring myself to look up.

Because I didn't want my mixed emotions to be readable all over my face.

The show was doing better than expected. The tickets for both sitting and standing spots were completely sold out, and there was even a waiting list if someone changed their mind.

Which no one ever did.

The booth to buy tickets opened at three PM, and for the past two days, people were lining up in the morning to get their chance at getting one.

There has never, in the history of this island, been a more popular attraction.

And I'm so proud and thankful to have been a part of it.

After Dres pulled his sweatshirt back on and began heading to the exit, I called out to him.

"Hey, wait."

He paused, then turned to face me.

I watched as his eyes met mine, then scanned over the rest of my body, as if he was seeing me for the first time. I was dressed in my best performance attire with my sleek black boots, my black mesh tights, and a tight, black crop top. Half of my wavy, red hair was pinned back, letting my face showcase my silver and black glittery makeup.

There was no way I was letting this look go to waste tonight.

I took a few steps to Dres, and in return, he took two long strides to me, meeting me halfway. His head tilted down to me with an amused look. His dark eyelashes accented his bright blue eyes, and I couldn't help but stare as they blinked at me curiously. He shoved his hands in his pockets as he waited for me to continue.

But before I could say anything, Vark stormed in through the back entrance. Both Dres and I turned to look, only to see a blazing, red-hot fury. Vark was seconds away from having steam blow out of his ears.

"What the hell, Dresden?"

Dres said nothing as his body remained relaxed, not caring in the slightest about pissing off his boss.

Vark motioned to me as if he was reminding Dres that I was here, available, ready to perform.

"Why aren't you using her?"

Dres gave a half-shrug. "I didn't need her tonight."

"I don't give a *fuck* if you need her or not. Use her."

I winced at his harsh words. *Use her.* I knew he didn't mean it in the way it sounded, but he could've picked his words more carefully.

Dres narrowed his eyes, and I knew he didn't like that choice of wording, either. "She needed a break."

What?

"She has fifty-one weeks to take a break," Vark spit out. "Now is not the time to leave her in the shadows. Chemistry sells. Romance sells. Sex sells."

My heart began to pick up the pace. Vark was right about all those things, but did we have those things? Did everyone else see what *I* felt?

Did Dres feel it, too?

"I don't think a lack of sales is our problem here," Dres countered, and I could feel my eyes go wide. He was fighting back.

Vark ignored the comment and continued his own train of thought. "From here on out, you will perform with her. You will use her for the last two shows. If you don't, I'll have both of you removed from this island. Utilize her presence. Understood?"

I nodded fiercely as Dres stood there, unresponsive.

Vark turned and walked back out, leaving the two of us alone backstage.

"Dres, listen. I'm sorry you're being forced to work with me, but I promise you, I'll do whatever you need from me. Even if it's just being your prop girl."

Dres turned to face me with confusion etched in his expression, and I continued.

"It's fine. I don't need a break, even though you think I do. But now we can figure something out for the both of us and finish the last two shows."

A heavy pause weighted itself between us, and then Dres did something that surprised me.

He took one final step toward me, closing the gap between us. I could feel the material of his sweatshirt brushing against my crop top with each breath we both took.

"You think I'm being forced to work with you?"

I cinched my eyebrows together, and now it was my turn to show confusion.

"I mean, yeah? That's what Vark was just yelling at, was it not?"

Dres shook his head, and I swore I could see a hint of a smirk playing on his lips.

"If I didn't want you here, you wouldn't be here."

I paused.

"But you're *here*, with *me*, because its exactly where I want you to be."

Holy shit.

I swallowed the admission down like a dry pill and took a sharp inhale, never letting my eyes fall away from his.

"I said you needed a break because it's true. You needed one. Everything that happens out on that stage is heavy, and it can fuck with you mentally. I don't want you stepping back out there until you trust me. I'm not doing *anything* until I have your full confidence in me."

My eyes remained locked with his as I absorbed his words.

He was protecting me.

He was *always* protecting me.

And if I didn't see it before, I saw it now.

I gave a subtle nod before letting a new smile spread on my lips. He didn't smile back, but instead, his eyes fell down to my lips, eyeing the shiny gloss that rested on the surface.

Then, he looked back up to me, and the new shimmer in his gaze lit an instant fire in the pit of my soul.

I could feel it.

The magnetic connection.

The harmony in our relationship.

The effortless balance between two beings.

Illusion

It was there, waiting for exposure.

And exposure is what it'll get.

My voice was heavy in my lungs but light on my tongue. "If you know what's good for you, you'll come with me," I said, then turned to go. Once I got to the back exit of the tent, I turned to look over my shoulder at Dres. He was standing there, watching me.

And then he actually did it.

He stepped to follow me.

And *that's* when he smiled back.

15

I held up the clear plastic bag to my eye level. The black and white fish swam quickly in its containment, with a slow and steady stream. I watched the wave of its black fins in the water, so effortless and fluent.

"It's a Dalmatian Molly," the employee stated, and I lowered the bag. With her arms outstretched to me, she handed me a clear glass bowl, a bubbler, some decorations, and a small tube of fish food. Thankfully, the booth workers always come stocked with necessities for those who actually do win a prize, since we're on an island and can't just find a nearby store to get what we need.

"That one looks to be a female," she added, her tone only slightly skeptical as I placed the small plastic bag inside the glass bowl. The fish floated, temporarily content with the inevitable travel.

Dres held out his hands, offering to hold everything, and I gladly handed over the bowl. He took it and raised it, trying to get a peek at the black and white spotted fish as well. A piece of me warmed at the sight of him doing something so simplistic as admiring a fish.

Then again, he's the one who threw the ping pong ball in the small cup of water, so technically, it was *his* fish.

Illusion

I only elbowed him three times, along with vocalizing my suspicions that he *had* to have used his magic to win, but he assured me he didn't.

I still didn't fully believe him.

"Congrats," the young, peppy booth worker said to both of us, and I gave her an easy smile.

"Thank you."

Dres echoed my thanks and we walked away, down the path of continuous booths. Everything was lit up and glowing with a radiance that only came once a year. Everything was alive. The sight of it all was alluring. The air had a special enticement to it, and I forced myself to feel the excitement and bottle it up for my memories.

The other fifty-one weeks of the year didn't hold a flame to this week.

Guests wandered the paths around us, popping balloons with darts, spraying small targets with squirt guns, and tossing plastic rings onto glass bottles. A few guests stopped and commended us—well, mostly Dres—on the show, but for the most part, everyone was stuck in their own little worlds and didn't bother to talk to us.

Because everyone was too busy looking happy.

There was an unexplainable bliss that knocked into you the second you stepped onto this island and the moment the week began.

I wasn't sure if Dres could feel it, too, but judging by his slow stride matching mine and his relaxed features, I knew there was something special he was feeling.

With the lights, sounds, smells? Yes.

With the island? Probably.

With me? *Maybe.*

With the glass fishbowl tucked under his elbow, he stepped alongside me. He turned to glance at me briefly before breaking the comfortable silence between us.

"She's yours."

I gave him a puzzled look in response.

"The fish. I want you to keep her."

I shook my head as a broad smile appeared from nowhere. "I don't think so. You won her. Plus, I don't have anywhere to put her."

Dres looked back down to the bowl, watching as the water in the clear bag waved with each step he took.

"Fine. But you have to name her. And feed her whenever I can't."

I narrowed my eyes at him in a playful defiance. "Fine," I answered, echoing his spat. "But give me time to come up with a name. It has to be a good one."

The corner of his lips turned up in a slight smirk, and my eyes dropped to it immediately. I could feel the ignite in my stomach, the brew in my bones, and the start of something I couldn't place.

My eyes found his again before quickly dropping my gaze back down to the ground.

"So, did you mean what you said back there?"

Now, it was Dres' turn to look at me with confusion.

"About playing a carnival game," I said, referring to a conversation we had before winning the fish. "You've really never played any?"

"Never."

"Have you ever *been* to a carnival?"

Dres shook his head, and my jaw dropped.

"What about a fair? Like, a local fair? County fair? State fair?"

His look was fleeting before shaking his head again. "No."

"Why not?"

And with that, he brushed me off. He didn't answer, didn't shrug, didn't give me any sort of reaction. He simply ignored the subject, and that was that. For once, I wasn't upset he was ignoring another one of my questions. Instead, I caught myself in wonder at the abrupt secrecy, but I also knew that things take time.

Trust takes time.

And if he wants me to trust him, I have to give him the same space to trust me.

So, I didn't push the subject, and I didn't ask again.

Illusion

After walking through the maze of walkways and getting a small cup of hot cider, we found ourselves close to the wooded area with our trailers. Dres nudged me slightly.

"I'm going to put the fish in my trailer."

I nodded, finishing the warm, seasoned drink and tossing the cup in a nearby trash can. "Okay. See you tomorrow?" I asked, but when I looked back, he was gone.

I turned around. Nothing.

I looked over my shoulder. Nothing.

Where the hell did he go? There was no way he could've disappeared that quickly.

But as I turned to look for him, my eyes landed on the Onyx, Twyx, and Thryx tents.

I tilted my head in piqued curiosity.

I shouldn't. I was already in the Onyx tent once this week; I didn't want to push my luck by going in again.

I didn't want to torture myself with the temptation to smoke while I was trying to quit.

Then again, I didn't have to go in *that* one.

My eyes skipped over the red glow of the Twyx tent and landed on the enticing stillness of the Thryx tent.

It was quiet. Too quiet. *Soundproofed.*

I took one final glance over my shoulder. Dres was still nowhere to be found.

He probably went back to his trailer before I could even realize he was gone.

So, since the night was only beginning, I headed toward the tent.

I lifted the heavy, thick tarp of the Thryx tent and allowed myself through. Candles were scattered all throughout the room, some high, some low, all giving off a light, floral scent and a luminescent glow. A trail of tea lights lined the floor in a guided path, leading in multiple directions to different areas. On one side was a circular couch, with at least ten people kissing each other, straddling each other, and fondling each other in all the right places. Some of them were completely nude, some only had a few pieces of clothing removed, and some remained fully clothed.

Whatever you felt like doing here is what you did. No one pressured you into anything you didn't want to do.

I passed the path to the circular couch and found myself watching a couple feed each other chocolate-covered grapes. The woman, who looked to be in her fifties, gently slid a grape into the man's mouth. He didn't look a day over twenty-one, but based on the grin on his lips and the heat in his stare, age clearly wasn't a factor for him, and he was enjoying every second. Another woman approached the pair and eased her way between the two. She faced the older woman, leaned in, and kissed her. The man wrapped his hands around her waist as he watched with lust in his eyes.

I stopped in my tracks as I watched the three of them enjoy each other.

The man must have noticed me, because his soft voice broke through the other noises in the tent. "Want in?" he asked, clearly not recognizing me as a performer.

I gave him a polite grin as I shook my head. He gave me a simple nod and turned back to the other two women.

God, if only Bram had taken my "no" that easily.

Along the back of the tent was a purple velvet couch. It was wide, it was deep, and it looked brand new. But, more importantly, it was empty. Candles lit the space around it, inviting me to relax in the sultry comfort.

Although the tent was soundproofed, the inside was surprisingly quiet. There were soft moans, hushed words, and muffled actions, but there was nothing harsh. There was no hostility, no aggression, no poison laced in anyone's actions.

It was safe.

Illusion

Of course, there were some people who enjoyed being loud, controlled, and dominated, and for that reason, the tent was soundproofed to the outside world. Those people can find their escape here as well, no questions asked.

But here, *right now,* the tent was as soft and sensual as it could be.

As I tried to crawl onto the purple, velvet couch, a strong arm wrapped around my waist and kept me from doing so.

My heart leapt into my throat at the sudden invasion. I quickly turned around, but the arm never fell from my waist.

Instead, it pulled me closer.

Dark, straight hair fell over his forehead as his bright blue eyes found mine in a stare so serious, so deep, that I couldn't help but tilt my head.

Dresden.

What was he doing here?

I could feel his tight chest breathing against my body as he held me close with one arm. My own arms were squeezed between us, so to make things a bit more comfortable and to give us more space, I moved my hands to his shoulders. I could feel him tense under my palms. My eyes moved down to the edge of his jaw, where I followed it to the curve of his lips, then back down to the sculpt of his throat.

Then, with his free hand, he placed the length of his index finger under my chin and directed my gaze back up to his.

Our eyes met again, and his stare was still as intense as before.

"What are you doing here?" I asked, a soft husk coating my words.

"I could ask you that as well," he answered, matching my lowered volume.

I looked at him, puzzled. "I'm here because I thought you went home for the night. And," I shrugged, "I'm here because I want to be here."

His eyes remained in their powerful state as he blinked once, his long eyelashes brushing against the dark freckle under his eye, and said nothing in return.

"How did you know where I was?" I questioned.

But before he could give me an answer, he lowered me down onto the velvet couch. My back rested gently on the surface as I let go of him and lowered my arms to my sides. His body hovered over me, his skin absorbing the minimal candlelight, his hardened jaw clenched in the stillness of the moment.

"Where you go, I go. What I gave you is mine."

I could feel the tightness in my chest grow.

What he gave me?

What did he give me?

A shot to the shoulder. A brush of death by drowning.

And then, it clicked.

The smoke.

When he breathed his smoke into my lungs, he was giving himself to me. I could feel it.

It was running through my veins. It was seeping into my core. It was infiltrating every part of me.

And I welcomed it.

But for some reason, with my body so accustomed to the constant battle of fight or flight, my protective side felt the need to fight it.

Because fighting back is what I'm used to. It's what comes naturally, and it's what I do best.

"Why are you here?" I asked again, this time with an unnatural snipe in my tone. "Why are you always diving into shit you don't need to be in?"

A look of hurt flashed over the glaze of his eyes, and I forced myself to ignore it.

"I don't need to be saved. You don't need to fight my battles for me. I can do this on my own. I always have."

His wounded expression remained, even as I continued.

"I've always been alone."

I could hear my voice crack as I lay under him, and my cheeks reddened at the embarrassing emotion that was floating to the surface.

Dres opened his mouth to speak, but I kept my defenses up and spoke before he could.

"Dres, you made it clear that I'm *only* your assistant."

He immediately shook his head. "You're not my assistant."

I paused, and I wasn't sure if I needed to roll my eyes or give in to the sinking, hopeful feeling that he was referring to something else. Something *more*.

"Right. Sorry," I assured. "Whatever it is, whatever we are, you don't need me. You don't want to use me. I get it." I made sure to keep my voice low while still getting my point across. I tried to sit up, but with a quick yet firm push of his hand, he kept me down. That hand then moved to the front of my throat, making no moves to grasp it, but instead, he caressed it. His touch was feather light as his long fingers trailed along the surface of my skin, tracing lines in a mindless pattern.

He shook his head again, keeping his vision on the hand that grazed my neck. "You're. Not. My. *Assistant.*"

And that's when I knew I was right in feeling the way I felt the first time.

This was no longer surface-deep. This was more.

I swallowed down my emotions, and his eyes watched the movement.

I struggled to bring my voice to an audible volume. "What happened, Dres?"

His eyes moved back to mine, and he gave me a quick look of confusion.

"The barrel. The water."

He dropped his gaze back down to his touch on my throat.

"Why don't I remember it?"

There was no answer on his tongue. There was no reply in his voice. There was only a weighted pause between the two of us, lingering in the flickering candlelight.

I quietly pressed again. "How did you heal my shoulder?"

His hand slowly slid up toward the underside of my chin, his knuckles grazing the smooth, tanned skin.

From the other side of the tent, the sound of a moan cried out, but it wasn't enough to tear either of us away from one another. We were locked on each other.

He had yet to give me an answer, and he didn't make any moves to leave. He was still hovering over me, his weight supported on his forearm next to me. My legs found the space between his, and I could feel the sides of his knees against mine.

And suddenly, the realization of our closeness dawned on me.

Dres' hand left my skin, letting the lack of his touch tingle in sensation, and moved to a lock of my red hair. He picked up a piece, felt it in the pads of his fingers, and studied its softness.

The glow of the candlelight framed his face flawlessly, with the gleam accenting the sharpness of his cheekbones, the chisel of his brows, and the seriousness in his expression.

There was something troubling him.

But what?

I wish I could switch places with him so I could know what he was thinking.

I moved one of my hands up to his forehead and brushed a piece of his dark hair to the side. But before I could finish the movement, his hand let go of my hair and moved up to stop me. He clasped my hand with his and lowered it gently, and his hair fell back to the spot it was before.

Our hands remained together, resting right below his chin.

He stared at me.

I stared at him.

And when his eyes fell back down to my lips, I knew it was in the cards for us. It was there, in that moment, waiting for us to take the opportunity.

There was nothing in our way but ourselves.

My heart was about to jump out of my chest. And based on the warmth of his hand and the speed of his breathing, Dres felt the same way.

And then, Dres got up.

He let go of my hand and pushed off the couch with the other.

I moved to sit up on my elbows as Dres stood back up to his full height. He briefly rubbed his bottom lip with his finger, unable to meet my eyes before turning away.

And as everyone continued kissing, feeling, and caressing each other, I watched as Dres left the tent, not sparing me a final look back.

16

The man I was staring at had one arm looped around the back of his head and the other arm tangled up and around his leg. He hobbled on his free foot, entertaining guests as they gawked at his abilities. I smiled to myself, enjoying the way Six was able to freely unhinge all his limbs with no pain and no repercussions.

One woman squealed out a mix of excitement and fear as Six switched legs quickly and effortlessly. His body was a puzzle to which only he had the key, and his abilities seemed to be endless.

The group of guests continued on as Six formed himself into a backbend and walked his way over to me.

"Hey, babe," he said while still upside down.

"Get up," I said through a laugh, and Six eased himself back into an upright position.

He swung one of his long arms over my shoulder. "To what do I owe the pleasure?"

I pulled the box of cigarettes out of my jean jacket and handed them over. "Take them."

Six glanced at me curiously before taking them slowly. "What's going on?" he asked with suspicion.

I grinned. "Nothing, stop being weird. I just think it's time for me to *really* try to quit."

Flashes of Dres filling my lungs with his smoke filled my mind, and a sudden chill ran down my spine.

Six held onto the box without taking his eyes away from me. There was a long silence. "Really?"

I shrugged. "I've been thinking about it for a while. It's just…" I struggled to find the words I wanted. "…not giving me any relief anymore. It's been doing more harm than good recently."

Six shook his head, giving me a smile while doing so. The look of admiration in his eyes was the justification I needed to believe I was doing the right thing.

"Good for you, babe. I'm proud of you."

And his words sealed it even more.

"Thanks, Six," I said, leaning into him. With his arm still around me, he squeezed my shoulders and pressed a kiss to the side of my head. "What else is new with you?"

He pocketed the carton of cigarettes as we walked, and I noticed he didn't pull one out to smoke. His consideration for me was not missed, and it gave me a small comfort.

"Not much new here. This week has been incredible so far. Everyone either loves or hates the things I do, but hey, a reaction is all I want. I don't care if it's good or bad."

There's the performative Six that I know. "I don't expect anything less from you."

"Link has been showing off more than usual, too. Him and his fucking ability to squeeze himself into a mailbox."

I burst out in uncontrolled laughter, knowing he was exaggerating. "A *mailbox*, Six?"

"Or, whatever. You know what I mean. He was pissing me off up until last night. When our shifts were over, he asked if I could bend backwards… on a bed."

I stopped walking to turn and face Six, my jaw dropping wide. "You mean…"

He smiled, and that made me smile. "Oh, yeah."

We both started to laugh, and before we could get carried away, I asked, "So, did you show him you can?"

"Willa, *baby,*" he said matter-of-factly, "what happens in the trailer, stays in the trailer."

The noise that came out of my mouth was a mix between a shriek and a laugh, and Six laughed with me. I didn't need to know any more than that, and everything he gave me led me to believe he was happy. And that's all that mattered.

We approached the wooden fence that led to the trailers. Instead of hopping over, we leaned against it.

I propped my elbow up onto the post. "Can I ask you something?"

"Of course."

"The second night," I started, thinking back to our second show. "You were there. You watched us. Did you see the whole show?"

Six nodded. "Yeah. Vark almost gave me shit for taking two breaks that night, but he knows I don't usually do that, so he let it slide."

I squinted my eyes in the sunlight that lit the sky behind him. "And you came in to see me afterward."

A puzzled look came over Six's face. "What's this about?"

A part of me wanted to lie, to make up something stupid about how I wanted to perfect the way it looked for future performances or something along those lines.

But this was Six I was talking to. He never let me believe I couldn't trust him, and he never gave me any reason to hide the truth.

So, the truth was what I was going to give him. Even if it was just a watered down version.

"I need to know what you thought of the barrel of water illusion, because that act took *a lot* out of me. More than I expected it to." I took a deep inhale at the understatement. "And everyone is complimenting us on it, but I'm having a hard time understanding why. From an audience member's point of view, what did you think?"

Six stared at me for a moment, unblinking, and I could tell he knew I was holding back a real reason.

But thankfully, he knew better than to push.

"Well, first of all, it was scary as fuck. But between you and sexy ass Criss Angel, you guys made it look effortless."

That got a small smile out of me, and he continued with the same smirk.

"You looked like you were really in trouble in that barrel. You played your fear beautifully. And then, when your body went limp and you looked like you passed out, I almost ran up there and pulled you out myself. Thankfully, Dres moved faster before anyone could reach you."

My heart was beating faster than I'd ever felt it. I recall getting into the barrel but can't remember *anything* after that. One second, I was holding my breath underwater, and the next, I was waking up on stage, under the lights and in front of a packed audience with soaking wet hair and clothes.

Six gave me a small nudge. "Hey, by the way, was that audience member in on it?"

I felt my eyebrows narrow slightly but stopped them before Six could catch my confusion.

"You know, the one that wanted to help you, but Dresden pushed him away?"

It was the same thing Bram mentioned to me in our previous conversation. I shook my head. "No. He wasn't."

"Damn, he thought you were really in trouble up there? So, then I wasn't the only one who thought you actually passed out, huh?"

I forced another smile. "I guess so."

I had no idea who he was talking about. I don't remember anything involving an audience member, but I know for a fact that Dres would never set up part of an illusion with anyone else. He worked alone, and he barely worked with me. That was it.

Six puffed out his cheeks and exhaled. "Well, whatever you guys are working with, it's incredible. You two have a lot going for you."

Pride bloomed in my chest. He was proud of me, and that warmed my heart.

Even though I had always excelled in the fact that I never needed anyone's approval, it never hurt to actually get it sometimes.

The wind gently brushed my hair across my face, and I pulled a hand out of my pocket to tuck it away. Although talking to Six about this was deemed useful, I needed more answers. The lack of understanding wasn't cutting it for me.

"I have to get back," Six spoke softly, hitching a thumb to the path behind him. "I'll see you around, okay?"

I nodded, still leaning against the wooden fence.

And with a simple look, it was like Six could read every thought that was hidden away inside of me.

"I don't know what's bothering you, but whatever it is, don't you dare let it consume you. Get out of your head and leave it all on that stage. You were made for this, Willa. There's no doubt about it."

And with a quick squeeze on my arm, Six turned and jogged back to the path. I watched him go, wondering why he had no doubts, and I had so many.

17

"You're on in thirty seconds," the stagehand whispered to me as I stood side stage. Once again, with no shock to me, the audience was packed full. It looked like there wasn't any room to even breathe down there. People were shuffling in their seats, fanning themselves as they waited for the performance to begin.

And with only a few more seconds to go, I felt a presence at my back.

I quickly spun around to see Dres there, grabbing his black sweatshirt at the back of his neck. I've come to realize that his outfit was the same every night- a plain, white t-shirt, dark, faded jeans, and old Vans sneakers that looked worn but not completely tattered.

With the final pull of the sweatshirt over his head, I watched as the material of his t-shirt climbed up with it. My eyes briefly fell to the exposed skin of his stomach, and my eyes quickly traced the defined lines of the muscles that dipped under his jeans. He tossed his sweatshirt onto a nearby chair, fixed his shirt, and ran a hand through his hair.

"Ten seconds," the stagehand noted.

Illusion

Dres took a step toward me, and our gazes locked. I could feel my pulse running in my throat at his closeness.

The last time I saw him was not even twenty-four hours ago, when he had me on the purple velvet couch underneath his body.

When he had his fingertips on my throat.

When his harsh words changed the night's trajectory.

"You're. Not. My. Assistant."

With every step closer to me, I could feel the draw of his body. His scent, his stare, his hunger.

I could see it.

And for a split second, he stopped. His stride came to a pause right in front of me as his eyes remained on mine. And in that moment, time stood still. I wanted him to pull me onto that stage with him. I wanted him to take my hand and lead me into the mystery.

But he didn't. He walked past me and onto the stage.

The crowd roared.

About twenty minutes went by with him and his tricks. I watched in awe as he created everything from nothing.

Smoke came from the floor.

Fire came from his palm.

Water floated in the air, suspended from gravity.

I still had no idea how he did *any* of it.

And then, right in the middle of his set, he turned his head and looked at me.

My heart fell into the pit of my stomach as his hand reached for me, palm up, waiting.

And a slight smirk curled the corner of his lips as I hesitantly walked out to him, taking his hand. My black ankle boots carried me into the light, my faux black leather tights shimmered with each step, and my bright red strapless bodysuit hugged my frame as I moved closer. It was another one of my favorite outfits, and I'm glad it was getting shown off tonight.

Dres' blue eyes shined in the glow of the spotlight as he watched me with an intensity I wanted to bottle up and keep. I could feel the lightning strike in the depths of my chest.

Once my hand was in his, he pulled me into him. Our chests met, body to body, as we both struggled to catch our breath. My face was only inches from his as I looked up, and he looked down, our hands still connected.

"Do you trust me?" he asked, his tone light and quiet for my ears only. His free arm wrapped around my waist, pinning my hips to his.

I blinked. Based on our past conversation, he wouldn't have brought me out here if I didn't.

And he was right.

In the beginning, I didn't trust him in the slightest. Of course, I didn't even know him—I still don't—but it was more than that. He scared me. He intimidated me. He led me into a state of confusion that I wasn't sure I could climb out of.

But night after night, he proved to be someone I could lean into. He fought for me; he *protected* me.

His eyes lingered on me as he waited for my answer. The audience was deafeningly quiet as they anticipated our next move.

I swallowed a new set of nerves as I whispered to Dres. "Yes."

His eyes watched me, my face, my expression for an elongated moment. It was like he was waiting for me to change my mind. But I wasn't going to because getting that *yes* out there was the truth.

It was heavy, it was significant, but it was the most important and true *yes* I could give.

And with that, I could feel his hands give me a gentle squeeze as he let me go.

Dres gave a single nod to a group of backstage workers who took that as their cue to bring out what was needed for the next illusion.

A few crew members rolled out a wooden arch. Along the top were two white ropes, equally spread apart and hanging from metal rings. Another crew member brought out two white sheets- thin enough to wave in the slight breeze but not thin enough to see through. They placed the sheets on the floor.

Oh, I knew this trick. Every magician in the world has attempted and mastered it. It was easy when done correctly, and it relied heavily on the performance rather than the "magic" itself.

It was a trick I could do and perform in my sleep.

But my nerves were still there, even if knowing the trick helped them settle a bit.

Dres guided me to the wooden arch with his hand on the small of my back. I stepped up on the makeshift floor and turned to face the audience, who all seemed to be watching intently.

With a soft, easy motion, Dres lifted my hand up, his own touch gliding up my forearm and landing on the underside of my wrist. He took the white rope, tied me into it, then moved behind me to my other side. He did the same with my other wrist, and both of my arms were lifted and secured.

At least, that's what it looked like to the audience.

In this trick, Dres was supposed to "tie" my wrists tightly, but in actuality, they were in slip knots that could easily become undone. All I had to do was wait until the sheet was raised and I was hidden from the audience, then I could slide out of the restraints and sneak away, giving the illusion of magic teleportation.

It was really just a simple redirection of attention.

Before the sheet was moved to cover me, Dres slid one hand to my jaw. He turned my head so I was looking at him.

And the stare he gave me spoke more than words ever could.

His eyes filled the depths of my desire. His passion radiated off of him and onto me. His gaze rattled every one of my instincts.

This was something different.

This was something otherworldly.

And just from his touch, I knew this wasn't going to go the way I had always known it to go.

Dres dropped his hand and backed away. He grabbed the white sheet in front of me and tossed it over the arch, covering all of me, top to bottom.

And when I tried to pull my wrists out of the ropes, nothing happened. I yanked on the material, but there was no give. If anything, it was squeezing my joint, causing my hands to turn a deep shade of red.

Shit.

A quiet whine escaped me as I pulled and pulled and pulled, pleading with the universe to somehow slip me out of these ropes. But nothing happened.

I was stuck.

Panic began to seep into my core at the realization that this illusion wasn't going to work. The sheet would fall and I'd still be here, embarrassingly standing in the same exact spot I was moments earlier. I would be the one to ruin the trick, screw up the performance, and shatter the magic.

The audience would be confused and definitely unimpressed, and it would be all my fault. And then Dres would probably hate me, too.

But maybe we wouldn't be in this mess if he simply kept me in the loop with his performances rather than taking me by complete surprise every time.

Leaning backward as much as I could, I peeked out from behind the sheet to look at Dres.

And sure enough, he was already staring at me, his eyes knowing and his expression sly.

He bent down to the floor and grabbed his own sheet, his vision still on me, quickly sending me a wink.

Trust, he mouthed to me silently, then turned his attention back to the audience.

My chest began to breathe heavily with each passing moment.

Inhale, exhale. Inhale, exhale.

This was going against everything I've known as a magician's assistant. The lack of rehearsal, the absence of communication, the reliance on *trust* and *only trust*. And since this was new territory for me, I couldn't help my nervous system from feeling the way it felt.

Fucking nervous as hell.

I gave a few more pulls on the ropes, hoping that they somehow loosened in the past twenty seconds. Of course, they didn't.

Thankfully, I was still shielded from the audience, so they couldn't see the inevitable alarm that was written all over my face.

And out of the corner of my eyes, I watched as Dres lifted his own sheet to cover himself from the audience. He wasn't tied up or hiding behind smoke and mirrors; he simply held the material in front of him.

And in that moment, I dropped my head down slightly, squeezed my eyes closed, and gave the ropes one final pathetic pull.

My heart climbed up into my throat as I feared opening my eyes. I didn't even notice that with the force of my last pull, my arms fell down to my sides. One second passed, then another, and another, before I heard an unusual sound.

It was applause.

I slowly opened one eye, then the other, and saw that I was no longer behind the sheet. In fact, I wasn't even on the wooden platform that I was a second ago.

I was on the stage.

Center stage.

With only my eyes, I glanced around. The audience stood to their feet, clapping and cheering as I remained motionless, even though all I wanted to do was stumble backward from the loss of feeling in my legs.

Holy shit.

How did I get here?

I brought my hands up and inspected them. Sure enough, there were red marks all around my small wrists. The skin was brushed and almost raw from where the ropes were rubbing me.

So, that part was real.

And in a new panic, I quickly looked around the stage for Dres. He was nowhere to be seen.

The sheet that *he* was just holding was in a pile at *my* feet.

I looked over to the wooden arch that I was in. The sheet was still draped over the top, and there was no movement coming from under it.

Without hesitation, I ran to it and pulled it down.

And there he was.

He was holding both ropes leisurely, his arms and wrists untied. He leaned his head against his bicep, almost like he was bored, unamused, and *waiting* for me to find him. He crossed one ankle over the other and gave me a half-smirk.

I wasn't sure if I wanted to punch him or smile.

Maybe both.

And at the sight of Dres unharmed and in my spot, the crowd roared even louder in ovation.

But Dres ignored them.

He effortlessly hopped down from the wooden platform and walked the one step that separated us. He wrapped his arm around my back, pulled me into him, and lifted my chin with his free hand.

I was too dazed to register his thumb's quick stroke over my cheek.

I was too disoriented to notice the pride that filled Dres' gaze to me.

I was too shocked to even comprehend the magic of the illusion, let alone accept it.

All I could hear was the continuous clapping from the audience as Dres dipped his mouth close to my ear, letting a single word escape from his full lips.

"Trust."

18

The nighttime breeze slid over my skin as I walked back to my trailer. Six had stopped me after the show, beaming with his usual pride. Even though he didn't get to see the show due to his schedule, he heard all about it almost instantly afterward.

Word spreads fast in the carnival, so it didn't surprise me.

And since I stood back to talk to Six, Dres was long gone before I had the chance to speak to him.

I wanted to say something, *anything*, but I wasn't sure where to begin.

Trust? Logistics? Believability?

There was *no way* I just teleported from one spot on the stage to the other.

It just wasn't possible. That's not how the world worked.

So, besides placing my faith in his hands, how else could I explain the magic that took place?

That's what I wanted to find out.

I pulled my white windbreaker closer to my chest. The night wasn't cold, but it was brisk enough for me to add a layer. The slight breeze wasn't helping the temperature, either.

When I approached my trailer, I noticed a soft glow coming from the lot diagonal from mine. Pops and crackles sounded from the back of the small area, and I knew exactly what I wanted to do.

Making my way over, I rounded the side of the trailer and went to the backside.

There was Dres, sitting in a folding lawn chair with a beer in his hand and a fire in the metal pit in front of him.

Staying still for a moment, I allowed myself to admire his profile. The way his dark hair fell perfectly along the sides of his head, the way his black sweatshirt spread tight across his wide shoulders, and the way his nose slanted straight, leading me in a trail to his lips.

And then I watched as he lifted the bottle to his mouth, his scabbed and bruised knuckles decorating the skin on his hand, and I was instantly thrust back into the moment.

My mind flashed back to the punches he threw for *me*.

The protection he gave for *me*.

The risk he dared for *me*.

It caught me off balance only for a moment before I righted myself again.

My mindless steps took me closer, and I glanced at the contained, dancing flames before turning back to him.

He didn't move to look at me, but based on the shift in his seat and the straightening of his spine, he knew I was there.

I broke the silence between us, speaking over the crackle of the burning wood. "Just so you know, Vark isn't a fan of us having fires during the big week."

Dres said nothing as he kept his gaze on the orange flames.

"It attracts guests' attention to the lots back here," I explained.

To be fair, Vark was probably busy doing other things. He rarely, if ever, made his way to the lots during the week. He had too many commitments and too many people to entertain to worry about anything happening back this way. So, my warning wasn't necessarily severe, but I figured I'd let him know anyway.

Dres seemed to have the same train of thought as me. His lack of eagerness to extinguish the fire let me know he couldn't care less about his boss and any rules that were set in place.

After another minute of quiet, I asked, "Is everything okay?"

And that's when Dres turned to look at me. His eyes met mine, and I could feel the dip in my stomach and the weight in my chest. His piercing blue eyes, his expressionless stare, and his relaxed demeanor all hit me suddenly.

Then, quietly and slowly, he stood to his feet. He left his beer in the cupholder of his chair and walked off to the side, into the darkness.

Where was he going? Was he leaving me here?

I heard some rustling in the tree line to the side, and I decided to give it a few more minutes before heading back to my trailer.

But thankfully, only after another minute, Dres came back hauling a wooden log. It was only about two feet long, but it was wide. He set it down on the ground next to the fire, perpendicular to the lawn chair he was previously sitting in.

Then, he surprised me. He sat down on the log, stretched his legs out, and grabbed the beer. Taking a quick swig, he motioned to the lawn chair. "Sit."

I obeyed.

The chair was actually really comfortable. The back tilted back a bit, and the metal frame didn't dig into my thighs like my lawn chair did. I rested my elbows on the armrests, exhaled, and looked at the glass bottle in Dres' hand.

"So, weed hinders you, but that doesn't?"

Dres gave a shrug. "No, it does."

I shot him a confused look, and he glanced down at the bottle, rolling it between his fingers.

"Everything that changes my state of mind hinders me."

And then he looked up at me, meeting my stare once again.

"Everything," he verified.

Everything.

The choke in my throat settled neatly in my neck, and I tried to swallow it down.

Our gazes locked, his ice-blue eyes seeping into me, melting me more than the fire beside us ever could. And in that stare, I knew he meant more than just drugs and alcohol.

"But sometimes, I don't care," he added, his eyebrows pinching together gently. "Do you want one?"

I shook my head. I wish I could muster out the words *thank you anyway,* but speaking suddenly seemed too hard for me.

Dres leaned forward, placing his elbows on his thighs toward his knees, his beer dangling in the space between his legs.

"Trust, right?" I asked, somehow finding my voice.

This time, he nodded once in confidence.

"My parents…" I began, even though my volume tried to trail off. I sat straighter and cleared my throat. "My mom and my stepdad, they weren't…"

I shook my head. I needed to try again. I kept my gaze down at my hands, unable to look at Dres while I spoke.

"I never met my dad. My *real* dad. He beat it before I was even born. My mom married my stepdad when I was young. He was the worst, Dres. The absolute fucking worst. He would get so mad whenever I wasn't home from school on time or whenever my grades weren't where he wanted them. He would slap me right across the face and then never apologize for it. And my mom just let it happen."

Lifting my chin, I looked up to the sky. The clouds were nowhere to be seen, and the stars shined above. I eyed them as I continued.

"She was getting it just as much as I was, I know it. She was probably getting more, honestly. But everything she got was behind closed doors. I heard the fighting at night, and I saw the bruises."

I blinked up at the sky.

"They matched mine."

Nothing but the sound of the crackling fire swirled around us.

"I started going out more, and then I just wouldn't come home for days at a time. I feel like it was better that way. I was out of my stepdad's hair and wasn't getting hurt. But because I had nowhere to go, I started skipping school, I started stealing, you know, typical stupid shit. I knew it was wrong, and I hated it, but I hated being home more. Then, one day, when I tried to come back, they had enough. They kicked me out and locked the door behind me. They left me outside and didn't let me in. My own *mother* wouldn't let me come back. I tried at different times of the day to find a way back in, but my stepdad always caught me and forced me back out."

I paused at the memories but refused to let them control my current emotions.

"I never understood why they hated me."

The last two words cracked in my voice, filtering a raw emotion from saying the one thing that devastated me out loud.

"Then, by some saving grace, Vark found me. I was waiting in the park for some of my friends, and they were either really late or they bailed on me. I'll never know because I went with Vark that day and never went back."

My eyes dropped to Dres, who was listening intensely to my story.

"Vark took me under his wing and brought me here. He told me I had potential, and I believed him because I was only sixteen."

Dres' eyes widened only a fraction, but it was enough for me to notice.

"Thank fucking God he never tried to cross any lines. I'm so thankful for that. But even though he didn't, other people did."

And that's when Dres dropped his head, letting it hang between his shoulders. He knew exactly who I was talking about, and he didn't need to ask for clarification.

Bram.

"But, don't get me wrong. This island is the best thing that could've ever happened to me. I found a place where I belong. I found something I love: magic. I have a place of my own, friends I see as family, and a week out of every year that brings me joy."

A slight exhale escaped my lips at the admission of my life. I had never told anyone the specifics of how I ended up here. I mentioned some things here and there to Six but never actually sat down and gave him the whole story. Bram never cared enough to ask, and even if he did, I don't think I would've ever told him.

There was something about Dres that allowed me to open up, and it wasn't the fact that he was trying to get me to trust him. There was an effortless connection with us, one that's origin I couldn't put a finger on. All he did was simply exist with me, and the melody of him was matched with the harmony of my soul.

Dres found my gaze once more, and I watched as his eyes shimmered in the glow of the fire.

I swallowed as my voice caught in my throat. "I love it here."

And I could've sworn I watched the corners of his mouth turn up in a slight smirk.

But as quickly as the look came, it fell. Dres took another drink of his beer and turned his stare to the slowly dying fire.

After a few minutes of quiet, with me inside my head wondering if I had overshared, a deep inhale found its way to Dres' lungs before he spoke. "It's been like this my whole life," he started, his voice completely catching me off guard. "Ever since I can remember, I've been able to do this."

I stared at him as I processed his words. "This?" I asked, confused.

"This," he echoed. With a quick lift of one of his palms, he held it face up toward the sky. Not a millisecond later, a flame erupted on his skin, matching the set of flames in the pit between us. It remained in the center of his palm for what felt like hours but was probably only a handful of seconds. Then, he closed his hand, and the flame died.

And all I could do was sit there, eyes wide and lungs tight, in complete awe.

Disbelief in my knowledge.

Uncertainty in my reality.

Confusion in my clarity.

Dres must've noticed my trepidation because, without second thought, he continued. "There has never been a time in my life where I couldn't do these things. My first memory is of me moving one of my toys without touching it. I could roll cars across the floor. I could create things that were never there to begin with. I could change people's memories or even erase them altogether."

I watched his lips as he spoke, the orange flames illuminating the side of his face.

"My parents took me to a facility called 'Practice of Limited Youth by Independent University Studies.' I'll never forget the name of that place; it's burned into my mind forever. Starting out, the visits were only once a week, but then it became more frequent, like once every few days. I didn't realize the place had significance, and I thought I was just playing in their playroom while my mom and dad did 'grown-up' things, but the truth was, they were watching me. Always. I never left their sight, even if it was behind a tinted window. And the doctors—the *scientists*—were always watching me, too."

A knot formed in my stomach, twisting my insides in dread. I knew where this was going.

"One day, when I was fourteen, I overheard my parents talking to one of the doctors, and that's when I found out that nothing was accidental. Everything was intentional."

My eyebrows instantly narrowed, and he continued.

"My mom was—well, more like *I was*—the product of an experiment. She was injected with a special serum while she was pregnant with me. To this day, I still don't know what it was, but when I found that out, it changed everything. I felt like some sort of mutant or a freak. Even my own parents looked at me that way sometimes, like they were scared of me. But *they* did this to me. I wouldn't be like this if it wasn't for them."

Heavy sorrow seeped into my bones from his words. "Dres…"

He shook his head, and it took everything in me to not reach over and place my hand on his arm.

"I held onto that anger even while I went through more shit throughout the years. It simmered inside of me, until one day when I was seventeen, I snapped. The doctors wanted to try to inject me with something to make me stronger, as if I wasn't enough of an experiment already. I told them no, but my parents tried to pressure me into it. I didn't give in."

We both stared at each other, still in the heaviness around us. It was Dres who finally broke the silence.

"That's when Hell broke loose."

My heart sped up in anticipation for his following words.

"They tried to pin me down and inject me, but I fought back. They tried to sedate me, but I fought back. My dad tried to tackle me into a chokehold, but I fought back."

Another pause, and the stare in his eyes turned from soft and gentle to fierce and serious.

"I fought back *hard*. And I don't regret any of it."

I swallowed, unable to move my eyes away from him.

"I killed him," he admitted. "I killed my own father with a quick snap of his neck. And on top of that, I wiped my mother's memory of me. She doesn't remember the fact that she ever had a son."

A gasp inched up the inside of my lungs, but I kept it hidden deep in my chest.

"I tried to kill the scientists, too, but for some reason, my abilities don't work on them. I couldn't wipe their memories, either. *Nothing* works with them."

The wood in the metal firepit cracked, but neither one of us flinched.

"I don't know if they're like me. I don't know if they have the same abilities I have, and I didn't stick around long enough to find out. I ran. If I couldn't kill them, there was no fucking way I was going to let them keep me as their science rat. And even though I couldn't beat them, I was faster. I was gone before they could even figure out what door I went through."

"Holy shit," I whispered under my breath. If Dres heard me, he ignored me.

"I've been on the run ever since. I haven't seen my mom since the day I fled. I don't know if anyone is even looking for me, but it's been about ten years, and I haven't been found. I've bounced around from place to place, making sure to not settle for too long. I've done odd jobs around the country and made enough money over time to keep myself alive. But no matter what, I always tried to stay under the radar as much as possible, and so far, it's worked for me."

My heart squeezed at the mention of his life and the unfair hardships he had to go through. Even as a kid, he had no choice in anything, and it broke my heart.

But the fact that he ended up here, on this island, where no one bothered any of us for fifty-one weeks out of the year, made things a little bit brighter. Reverie Island was like a silver lining.

It was perfect for him.

Secluded, but not alone.

Suddenly, I felt optimistic about him staying here on this island. He would be safe here, with us.

No one could catch him. And if anyone tried, he had a new family to back him up and protect him. He was one of us.

Leaning forward, I grazed the back of his hand with my touch. He didn't react with more than the flicker of his eyes to mine, but I didn't mind. I loved the feel of his skin under mine, and the fact that he didn't pull away spoke volumes.

"I like having you here, Dres."

He made no moves to respond, but his eyes locked onto mine for what felt like an eternity. The fire warmed my side, and I leaned closer to Dres, sitting on the edge of the lawn chair. I brushed the back of my hand against his, the valleys of my knuckles skimming along the cuts and scrapes of his, and I swore I felt him lift his hand ever-so-slightly in return.

Illusion

Dres' voice was deep and rich when his words left his lips. "Come with me."

19

Dres and I walked side by side down the narrow stone path. There were still many guests walking about, exploring the grounds, but it was getting late, and you could tell a lot of people had turned in for the night. They headed back to their luxurious tents, settling in before the final full day tomorrow.

The scent of freshly roasted almonds filled my nose as we passed Troy's tent. I glanced inside to see him and his wife working hard, filling gift bags with their most popular snack. My mouth began to water at the sight and sweet aroma of my favorite treat.

Without a second thought, I headed inside, pulling Dres in with me by his elbow. Wherever Dres was taking me could wait.

"Hey, sweetheart!" Troy exclaimed with beads of sweat dripping down his temples. "I hear nothing but wonderful things about your show. I wish I could see it."

I gave a full, sincere smile. "Thanks, Troy. I wish you could, too."

He nodded to the display case that was slowly filling with bags. "Grab one. My treat," he ushered to me while having his hands full.

Leaning around the glass, I reached in and grabbed two bags, keeping one and handing the other to Dres. He took it and studied the bag.

"You work harder than anyone else here," I began, speaking to Troy as I pulled out some extra cash from the pocket of my windbreaker. "You're not giving me free stuff."

I placed a twenty-dollar bill on the counter, and Troy gave me an appreciative grin. "Have a good night, you two."

His eyes bounced from me to Dres, then back to me as he tipped his chin in approval. Dres and I headed back out to the tent before I heard Troy call out to us.

"No way, sweetheart. This is five times the amount I charge."

We both stopped to glance over our shoulders. Troy was at the glass counter, holding up the bill I had just laid down.

But behind it…was another twenty.

My forehead instantly scrunched as I furrowed my eyebrows in confusion. Did I accidentally put another twenty down? I swore I only had one in my pocket.

My hand checked the inside of my windbreaker. Sure enough, it was empty. I didn't remember putting more down, but maybe…

I shot Dres a glance, who was already staring at me. And with that stare was the most genuine smirk I've ever seen on him. He sent me a quick wink, and that's how I knew.

Dres added that money, just like how he put the four dollars in my pocket.

He really wasn't kidding when he said he could do these things. I never doubted him, but to see him do it with my own eyes was a constant confirmation.

I gave Troy one final smile before continuing our exit. "Bye, Troy!" I said with a slight laugh. Troy really deserved it. He and his wife were the sweetest people on this island, and their almonds were nothing less than perfect. Every penny they made was well-earned, and I always believed they should be making more. If I could have a hand in that, I would.

As we were leaving the tent with our small bags, someone was entering. We almost collided, but I froze instead.

I glanced up to cold eyes that I knew so well.

Bram.

His dark hair was pulled back into his signature low bun, which was frayed and messy. He was sweaty, out of breath, and looked dirty. His solid, white cast still cradled his right wrist, and his left eye had a giant purple circle around it, accentuating the bags under both eyes.

He looked like a mess.

And it was obvious that there was more than one cause for this downfall.

As soon as our eyes met, he blinked once and looked away. I could tell he wanted to say something, but he knew better. Instead, he lingered in front of me for only half a second before moving around me and heading into Troy's tent, ignoring me altogether.

Did I feel bad for him? No. Did I miss him? Hell no.

Did I worry about him? Maybe a little. But why? He deserved everything he got.

The punishment from Vark, from Dres, and from me.

But he and I were a team for so long. We were always as one, even if our dynamics weren't always equal. He had my back. At least, for the longest time, I *thought* he did.

But he also had my body, even if I didn't give it to him.

He took it.

"Suck, Willa."

He *stole* it.

I exhaled through a shudder, and I could feel Dres stiffen next to me.

"No."

I turned to look at him, processing the meaning of the single word he said to me.

Dres' expression was hard, his eyes piercing and his voice low but harsh.

"Don't."

Dres didn't need to explain himself. I knew exactly what he meant with those simple words.

Don't worry about him. Don't think about it. Don't turn back now.

And I didn't.

With another half-smile to Dres, I kept walking. Within a few steps, Dres caught up, and we both acted as if we saw nothing.

I could acknowledge that Bram would always be around, but I wouldn't let him be in the center of my life anymore.

He was out. For good.

I opened my clear bag and tossed a couple of almonds in my mouth. This was my third bag this week, and I wasn't complaining. Not only did it taste good, but it felt good to have something replace the constant flow of cigarettes I was used to.

"So, how's Jane?" I asked through the bites of the almonds.

Dres popped an almond from his own bag in his mouth, then gave me a puzzled look. "Jane?"

I smirked. "The fish."

"That's the name you chose? Jane?"

I nodded.

"Why Jane?"

I gave a slight shrug as we continued walking, with Dres leading the way. "Because I like Breaking Benjamin. And I thought it was cute."

Dres let out a hum of understanding. "So, does that mean I have to get her a diary?"

I almost stopped in my tracks, but instead, I whipped my head to look at him. "You know Breaking Benjamin?"

Dres let out a small chuckle, lighting me up. "Just because I've been off the grid doesn't mean I'm oblivious. I like music."

He likes music. Out of all the conversations I've had with him so far, that's the first thing he's ever mentioned liking. *Music.*

And based on the next few almonds he threw in his mouth, I assumed he liked those, too.

I couldn't help but smile to myself as warmness spread throughout my entire being.

We continued to walk together, weaving through the guests.

"So, where are you taking me?" I asked, retying my bag and shoving it in my jacket pocket.

Dres finished his almonds and nodded up to the two tents ahead. One was the palm reading and tarot card tent, and the other was the tattoo tent. Both were open and illuminated, and a handful of guests lingered around them. Two round tables were fixed inside the palm reading tent, and both were occupied. Inside the tattoo tent were three massage tables, with a guest lying on two of them. The third was empty.

Either we were about to learn our future, or draw our future in our skin.

I had an idea of which one.

And as Dres led me to the tattoo tent, I guessed correctly.

The free tattoo artist glanced up at us. He had tattoos all around his neck and face, piercings in his lips and nose, and giant gauges in his ears. Although the average person would deem him scary, he beamed a warm, refreshing smile at us.

"Holy shit. You guys are the magicians."

Dres stood with his hands in his pockets and gave a single nod.

"You guys are incredible. I got to watch the show the other night, the one with the water."

The water. The barrel.

I still wasn't entirely sure what had happened.

I gave the most authentic smile I could muster, and I prayed that it didn't come off forced. But judging how the tattoo artist seemed at ease, he must've not noticed.

"I'm Wes." He stuck out his hand, and we both shook it. "You guys want something done?" he asked, pulling out a sheet of small flash designs. "I can do one of these, or I can try to draw something up."

Just as I was about to look at the little pictures on the paper, I saw Dres shake his head out of the corner of my eye.

"I was actually hoping I could try something," Dres said, surprising both me and Wes. "Can I have an hour?"

"An hour?" Wes echoed with a deep hesitancy. "I don't think that's a—"

Dres cut him off. "It's nothing crazy. Trust me."

There it was again. Trust.

It was like those words unlocked something in anyone who heard them come out of Dres' mouth. A switch was flipped, and Wes stood up to his feet.

"Alright, sounds good. I'm starving anyway, dude. The hour is yours. I'll be back."

And with a quick pat on the back to Dres, Wes was gone. He walked into the crowd and headed toward the food tents.

I glanced to Dres with wide eyes, unable to comprehend anything that had just happened. I couldn't comprehend anything that happened this entire week, actually.

He continues to surprise me.

"Lay down," Dres commanded, and I tilted my head at him. He looked serious but comforting at the same time.

"On my stomach or back?"

"Stomach."

After taking off my windbreaker, I climbed up on the table and lay facedown. I moved my arms to my side and let my cheek rest on the surface, my face aimed in Dres' direction.

He sat in Wes' chair and scooted it to me.

He and I stared at each other for a few moments, the heat between us intensifying with each passing second. His blue eyes flickered back and forth on mine as he slowly moved his hand up to my back. His touch grazed my skin softly as his knuckles brushed the upper part of my spine.

It was the kindest, most compassionate touch I've ever felt from another human being, and it made my heart thump a little harder.

His fingers trailed down to my corset bodysuit. He undid the top button, then looked back into my eyes for consent. I blinked and nodded, allowing him to continue.

He undid the rest of the buttons, his hands brushing each part of my skin as he made his way down the row.

And when my corset was completely undone, he opened it, letting the fabric fall down at my sides. My back was completely exposed, and the chill of the air layered on my flesh, creating a cluster of goosebumps.

I watched Dres the entire time. His eyes scanned me, studied me, and memorized the curve of my upper body. Something different swept over his expression, and for a moment, I couldn't place it.

Suddenly, Dres cleared his throat and slid the chair back to the desk with all the supplies. He pulled on latex gloves, replaced the needle in the tattoo gun, and poured out a little bit of black ink.

"Have you done this before?" I asked with my cheek still pressed to the padded table.

"Never."

I narrowed my eyes. "You seem awfully familiar with all this."

Dres dipped the needle into the ink. "Like I said, I'm not oblivious. One of my odd jobs was helping out at a tattoo shop."

A lock of his dark hair fell over his forehead, and my eyes trailed the movement. His mannerisms were so effortless, so fluid, it was like he didn't have a care about anything. He didn't stress. He didn't ever seem stiff. It was as if his soul was free.

He moved back to me and hovered over my side. His gloved hands rested along the back of my ribcage, and he spared me one final glance.

"Do you trust me?" he asked, a small smirk forming on his lips.

The buzz of the tattoo gun rang through the air. A piece of me was nervous, only because I had never gotten a tattoo before. It wasn't because I didn't know what he was about to put on me, or if he could even draw. My only fear was the pain and nothing else.

Then again, I recently had an arrow pierce through my shoulder. I'm sure I could handle a tattoo.

My eyes flickered back to his, and I caught the sparkle that hinted against his light blue irises.

I trusted him.

"I do," I whispered, and Dres' smirk turned into a fully formed smile.

And I never felt safer.

Moments later, I felt the sharpness of the needle in my skin. It was uncomfortable, but it wasn't nearly as bad as many people make it out to be. I tried to follow the tracing in my mind and figure out what he was etching into my skin, but I lost the outline in my mind after about twenty seconds.

The silence between us was more than comfortable. I didn't feel the need to say much, and he didn't either. I went back and forth between closing my eyes and letting my body rest, to watching him concentrate on the task at hand. He looked so focused, so fixated on getting this done and done right, and I admired it. I admired him.

I liked the way he was fearless and how he brought that same fearlessness out of me.

I felt a sudden coldness on my skin, and I realized he was wiping off the smeared ink with a soapy paper towel. Once the area was sufficiently clean, he leaned back down and continued tattooing.

It was then that I had a lingering question on my mind. My lips parted as I struggled to squeeze the thought out, concern floating in my nervousness that it would be a stupid question.

My eyes traced the frame of Dres' face from the straight line from his nose to the fullness of his lips, from the path of his jaw to the shadows on his throat.

And as I watched him intently, he didn't look up from my skin as he muttered aloud, "Yes?"

My heart skipped. He knew I was watching him, and he knew I had a question on the tip of my tongue.

He raised his eyebrows as he studied my skin.

My eyelids fluttered as I whispered. "Do you even know my name?"

Dres paused, and the tattoo gun went silent. I immediately regretted asking because the second the thought left my lips, I knew it sounded dumb.

But even through the regret, I couldn't help but wonder because he has never called to me before. He has only ever reached for me with his hand and searched for me with his eyes.

He briefly glanced to me, his head barely tilting at my words.

"Willa," he said with a deep husk coating the name. *My* name.

It was the very first time he had ever said it.

And I'd be lying if I said it didn't do something to me.

Dres continued the tattoo as I tried to catch my breath, the volume of my voice lowering with my impending admission.

"Willa Wolfe," I began, trying to distract myself from the slight pain in my side. "It's my name *here*, but it's not my real name."

With his curiosity piqued, Dres glanced up momentarily, acknowledging that he was listening.

"No one here knows my actual name. I changed it so in the very off-chance my parents ever came in contact with me again, they wouldn't be able to call me by name."

Not that they ever would, because doing so would require them to come to the island as guests, which they could never afford.

But, as the phrase goes, never say never. Who knows, they might be filthy rich by now. So, with that chance always lingering in the back of my mind, I knew I had to protect myself the moment I decided to leave my old life.

Thus, Willa Wolfe was born.

And in trusting Dres, I gave him the reserved truth.

"As far as anyone knows, Chloe Renowski is dead."

I said it so seriously that Dres didn't reply with his voice, but only with the solemn look in his eyes. He had nothing to add, nothing to counter with.

Illusion

It felt good to get it out in the open to *someone*. No one knew. Not Bram, not Six, not even Vark. The second I got into that car with him, he told me I could be whoever I wanted to be.

And that was the day that Chloe died for good.

After I left my secret in the space between us, more silence floated by, and it was peaceful. The guests at the other tattoo tables had left, and the respective tattoo artists cleaned up and left for a break, leaving just me and Dres in the tent.

Judging by his posture, he seemed like he was close to finishing the tattoo. He cleaned the ink again with another wet, soapy paper towel, and I watched how naturally he moved.

I looked at him, puzzled. "Do you have any tattoos?"

With the way he poured the ink into the little cup and checked the needle in the gun so carefully, he was too familiar with the setup and process to *not* have one, right?

Dres immediately stiffened at my question, and I noticed that he refused to look at me anymore. His eyes remained locked on my tattoo as he continued to clean it attentively. He pulled off his latex gloves with a snap, threw them away, and rested his hands on his thighs.

"All done," he said, and I didn't miss the way he ignored my question.

Slowly, I sat up. Keeping my hand planted on my chest, I held the corset against my skin, covering me as I hopped off the table. There was a mirror along one of the tent's curves, and I walked over to it. I turned myself to see my first tattoo, located on the left side of my back. It was red and slightly swollen, but the black lines were unmistakable.

It was one single stem, with four little flowers trailing up and two tiny leaves on each side toward the bottom.

It was dainty, it was tasteful, and it was *so* cute. I fell in love with the simplistic design instantly.

"Dres," I exhaled, then turned to face him, my eyes wide with appreciation.

He leaned forward in his chair and rested his elbows on his knees. "They're forget-me-nots."

I turned back to the mirror and glanced at the tattoo in adoration. "I love it."

While admiring the tattoo, I didn't register that Dres had gotten up from the chair and walked over to me. I didn't see him until I saw his reflection in the mirror.

He approached me until he was directly behind me. While looking at him through the mirror, I watched as he brought one hand up and traced the fresh tattoo with his fingers. Just like before, his touch was so delicate, his fingertips soft on my skin. His other hand snaked around my front and found my jaw, his thumb gliding the length of the bone.

I relished the sensation of his skin on mine. Intimacy filled my core as I watched him caress me in the mirror, his touch lingering on me in an act so passionate and fervorous. Succumbing to him, to all of him, I let my eyes fall closed in heat.

And when I opened them only seconds later, I followed the trail his hand created as he ran over the length of the tattoo. A new, surface-level heat scorched my skin, and I watched as it went from red and inflamed, to pink and irritated, to completely normal and healed.

Healed.

The image of the forget-me-not rested under my skin, but instead of the fresh pain, it was entirely recovered.

My chest heaved in astonishment as Dres continued to brush against my skin, savoring the feeling under his touch. His head dipped down to my ear as his breath layered over my sudden onset of goosebumps.

I turned away from the mirror to face him, and his other hand never moved from my face. Our eyes locked, his jaw hardened, and there wasn't a fearful bone in my body.

His hand slid under my red hair and down to the nape of my neck. I let my head tilt back an inch, watching as he and I lingered in the fragile moment.

Illusion

While still holding my corset against myself, I moved my other hand up to his chest, feeling his hard body. It was as if we had the same track mind, and there was no need for words to pass between us.

Because we knew.

We were a team.

We had the trust within us.

20

Our moment was shattered when Wes came back to his station, breaking us away from any intimacy we had created.

"You guys good?" he asked, and we both turned to look at him. He took a sip of his drink with his straw.

"Yeah," Dres answered flatly, then quickly moved around me to my back. He grabbed the edges of my corset and clipped them back together, his knuckles once again brushing against my chilled, previously exposed skin.

One more graze of his fingertips, and my heart would combust. Easily.

Once he was done, he grabbed a hundred-dollar bill from his pocket and handed it to Wes. I smiled at the fact that he didn't make it suddenly appear or leave it on the desk, but he actually gave it to Wes in a thankful, thoughtful gesture. What it was for, I wasn't sure.

For letting us use the station and all of his equipment?

For leaving and giving us privacy?

Whatever the reason, I was thankful that Dres was appreciative. Then, in that next moment, he took me by surprise by grabbing my hand and leading me out of the tent. I followed closely, my feet leading me while my mind hyper-focused on the feeling of his warm hand in mine. On my way out, I quickly grabbed my windbreaker and said bye to Wes, who didn't seem to care about us leaving or staying.

As soon as we stepped out of the illuminated tent, our hands disconnected, even though I was mentally begging for it back. I pulled on my jacket and zipped it up.

With our aimless steps and hushed intimacy, we walked back into the main grounds. More performers danced in the paths around us.

A man on a unicycle squeezed between me and Dres.

Two trapeze gymnasts swung above us, catching each other with no net below.

A young man leaned against a nearby tree with a single, dim spotlight shining on him. A group of guests circled him as he twirled a sword around, balancing it with his index finger alone. He caught the handle, flipped it vertically, and shoved the sword's blade down his throat with ease. The group of guests swooned with astonishment.

Right as we passed one of the popcorn tents, a woman with a torch clutched in her palm skipped in front of us. Her white, sparkling tank top and skirt shimmered under the lights, the material contrasting against the animated night.

With a bright smile, she exhaled a gusted breath against the torch, blowing a giant flame in the path before us.

Dres and I both laughed at the sudden excitement. The woman skipped around us, blowing more fire as she twirled in her steps. She paused in front of us, threw her fire stick up in the air, and caught it gracefully.

I shook my head in disbelief. Some of these performers were so damn impressive. There was no way I could ever do that, no matter how hard I practiced.

Some things just come naturally to people.

Dres spoke up next to me, a coy smile on his lips.

"You missed some."

He raised his hand, revealing a controlled fire in his palm. The performer stopped in her tracks, watching Dres with wide eyes.

The orange flame danced briefly before he aimed his palm at the unlit end of her torch. The wood blazed instantly, casting both sides in a warm hue.

The woman tossed the stick in the air while giving it a spin. She caught the bare center of the baton as if she'd been doing this her whole life.

She probably has.

With a final wink to both of us, she skipped away with her double-fire torch. She was part of what made the week so magical, and I found myself disappointed that it was almost over.

One more night, and then it would be another year before I could experience it again.

As the woman trotted away, Dres closed his hand, taking his fire away with it.

It baffled me that he could do these things whenever he wanted.

With no one around, he could execute things that nobody could ever dream about. I warmed at the idea that I didn't have to wait between years to experience *his* magic.

"Hungry?" he asked, snapping me out of my thoughts.

I tilted my head. "Kind of?"

Without another word, Dres jogged into the nearby tent, only to come back out a minute later.

In his hand was a small paper cup, and in the cup were popcorn kernels.

I glanced down at the cup, then back up to Dres. He returned the intrigued stare with his eyebrow cocked.

Then, reaching in, he grabbed a kernel and pinched it between his thumb and forefinger. It was only a few seconds before it popped, revealing a perfectly popped piece of popcorn.

There was his magic again, but this time, it was for my eyes only.

Moving his hand to me, he offered me the popcorn, and now it was my turn to give him something for *his eyes only*.

Instead of taking it with my hand, I grabbed his wrist gently and guided the popcorn to my lips. I opened my mouth and took the food gently, easily, and slowly. His eyes watched the movement, tracing the way my tongue just barely grazed his warm fingers.

I chewed the piece of popcorn and swallowed, and Dres didn't blink once.

"More?" I asked with hooded eyes.

Dres reached in, grabbed another kernel, and popped it.

A sly smile spread on my lips as I leaned down again, teasing him with a seductive stare. But this time, instead of taking it with my mouth, I snatched the piece of popcorn away with my hand.

"Open up," I commanded with a laugh. Dres released a wide smile and obeyed, dropping his jaw down. I tossed the popcorn into his mouth, and he caught it. He chewed and swallowed, all while popping more popcorn with his hand.

"Open up," he echoed the same order to me, but before I could try to catch the food, he tossed the popcorn at my face. We both burst out in uncontrolled laughter, and I lunged for him and his snack. Trying to hide his popcorn, he turned away, and I jumped onto his back, reaching for the paper cup.

"I don't think so," he teased with another laugh. I managed to grab a handful of popped popcorn before the rest spilled everywhere, getting all over us and the ground below. I could feel a couple of kernels fall into my boots and roll against my ankles.

I took the popcorn in my hand and pushed it into Dres' mouth, and his muffled laughter against my hand had me grinning from ear to ear.

It was a smile I didn't have to force, and I didn't realize how good it felt until my cheeks started to ache.

"Alright, *alright,*" he surrendered through the crunch of his chewing. I slowly slid off his back, highly satisfied that I won the popcorn battle.

I titled my head up with a proud grin, and Dres returned the playful cockiness.

"This isn't over," he told me, his light-hearted threat clear. I watched as he wiped the popcorn crumbs off his face and sweatshirt, his smile never fading.

Oh.

Oh, that *smile.*

I could feel my heart thump against my ribs. It was a *good thump.*

I'd never felt a good thump before.

Dres must have noticed my pause because when he looked back up to me, he matched my locked stare.

The stare that we've both mastered, the stare that wasn't shared with anyone but us.

This was definitely something more than *just magic.*

He cocked his head to the tree line, motioning to our trailers. "Let me take you back."

I nodded, and we headed back to the trailers. It had to be the middle of the night, maybe around two or three, and my exhaustion was beginning to hit me full force. I let out a yawn, and then another, before Dres noticed. His lips turned up in a small grin before he turned back to the path.

We hopped the fence, and it was only another minute before we came up to my trailer. We approached the door, and Dres opened it for me. I headed inside, then turned to him before closing the door.

"Should I even bother asking about tomorrow? Uh, I mean, tonight?" I asked, holding the door open.

Dres gave me the blank look that I knew so well. "What do you think?"

"I think..." I began, but then I really started to think. We've made it this far with me completely in the dark. We soared in performance as I went in blind every night. We fed off the rush, both from the act and from each other.

Why stop now?

"...Never mind," I finished, keeping all my thoughts inside. To be honest, I've come to love the rush he gave me. I enjoyed the way the shows ended up. I appreciated how the audience reacted, the excitement of my discoveries, and the unknowns of the magic. I drank the adrenaline like water in the desert.

And what surprised me even more was that I knew Dres would tell me what he had planned if I asked. Because, at this point, if I didn't have faith in him, all our hard work together would have been for nothing.

"Thank you," I said, my voice tired and eyelids heavy. "For tonight."

Dres shook his head. "Goodnight, Willa."

His steps carried him away, around the back of my trailer and towards his own. Before he could completely vanish out of sight, I shouted to him. "Tell Jane I said hi. Give her some extra food for me."

With his hands in his pockets and the hood of his sweatshirt lining his neck, he turned and gave me an authentic smile. It felt like a sword to the stomach, and I couldn't help but feel a tiny bit of disappointment as I watched him go.

Because I didn't *want* him to go.

The realization hit me hard.

I felt myself longing for his mystery, for his presence, for the safety he makes me feel.

I was longing for *him*.

21

The final night.

The anticipation was unreal.

Peeking out from behind the curtains, I watched as guests filled the entire tent. We were completely sold out in every way. No seats available. No standing room available. Guests were outside the tent, trying to glance into the gaps of the tent's fabric. Some people even snuck in to sit on other people's laps.

We were *that* good of a show.

Butterflies thrashed inside me as I waited for our cue.

I wanted to walk with Dres to the show, but I gave up waiting for him to pass by my trailer. I sat on the front step for hours, hoping to catch him on his way. But once the clock reached ten minutes 'til show time, I couldn't bear to wait much longer. I was cutting it close enough as it was.

Now that there was only one minute before the show, my nerves electrified every inch of my body as I waited for him to show.

And, sure enough, I felt him before I saw him. His presence was at my back, and I turned to see him.

He pulled his sweatshirt off, tossed it aside, and rushed to me. My heart sank down into the depths of desire as he grabbed me, his hand finding the back of my neck, just like he did last night.

I thought of the tattoo he gave me. It was a permanent reminder of him, our shows, and how he brought me out of the shell I didn't know I was in.

His eyes found mine as his free hand wrapped around my back, pulling me harder into him.

This was it. This was our last show together until next year. I etched this moment into my brain.

The final seconds before the greatest magician I've ever known walked out on that stage.

My heart surged with excitement and pride, both in him and myself.

His hand moved from my neck to the side of my face, and my head leaned into his touch, my skull cradled in the cusp of his hand.

My eyes fell closed. There was nothing that could keep my heart out of this moment.

"You're on," the stagehand whispered, and I was proven wrong. My eyes snapped open, and I saw Dres watching me.

His face was tight, contemplation filling each inch of his skin, and his gaze said it all.

His arm remained wrapped around my back, pinning me to him as his body heat covered both sides of me.

Seconds passed as our eyes remained stuck on each other, unable to find something else to look at. All we had was this.

All we had was now.

"You're *on*," the stagehand hissed in anger.

Dres' arm slowly dropped from my back while his other hand slowly brushed along the side of my face. It lingered there for a second, and then another, before he dropped that one too.

And then, he walked out on stage.

The air that grazed my skin from his departure wasn't cold, but it sure felt like it compared to his warmth. I remained facing the backstage area as I heard the roar of the crowd erupt at his entrance. And I knew, without looking, that the audience was the last thing he cared about.

He didn't need the show. He didn't need the attention.

Magic was in his blood, Reverie Island or not. It would always be in him, no matter what.

So the appeal that shines through him and onto the audience wasn't necessarily a front, but it definitely wasn't what it seemed, either. It wasn't an illusion.

There was no mystique.

It was simply…him.

Finally gaining the courage, I turned to face the stage. Dres had already begun his tricks, captivating the audience in awe and complete disbelief.

And even though I had seen some of these tricks before, there was still astonishment running through me, taking me, hypnotizing me.

There were even some shouts from the crowd of "There's no way!" and "Do it again!" all of which Dres tuned out. He kept his focus on the enchanting spirit inside of him.

Because that's all he needed.

He didn't need the rush of the crowd. He didn't need the approval of others.

He wouldn't be him if he did.

With only minutes left of his set, Dres turned to look at me, and I knew that was my cue.

But before I could even step foot onto the stage and into the light, Dres came walking over to me. I froze because it was something he hadn't done before. Normally, his look was a cue for me to go to him, but this time, he came to me.

He stepped behind the curtain slightly, his backside still visible to the crowd. Moving his hand back up to my cheek, his thumb brushed against my soft, highlighted skin.

"My Willa," he rasped, and I almost crumbled right there.

Illusion

It was the third time he had said my name, and it didn't feel any less significant.

In fact, with the possessive noun in front of it, my name seemed to have a whole new meaning to him.

My eyes glistened with a new emotion as I followed him out onto the stage. With my bodycon black dress that came down mid-thigh, matching black tights, and combat boots, I felt beautiful as I walked onto that stage.

And with Dres walking backward, my hands grasped in his, his eyes raked over every inch of my body.

It was passionate.

It was heart-stopping.

It was everything I had ever wanted.

His eyes held a warming emotion as his lips curled up into a delicate grin. One that the audience couldn't see, one that was shared only between us.

It was *only us*.

Without any direction from Dres, the backstage workers brought out the setup for our final act together. I glanced over to the prop to see a black metal platform with one giant spear in the middle. It was pointing up, with the tip at the very top.

I knew this illusion. I had performed it in the past.

And this time, I knew it wasn't about to be done in the same way as before.

My hands pulled away from Dres as my palms found my stomach. I brushed along the flat fabric of the dress, smoothing it down.

I don't have what's needed for this. I don't have the structure for the pipe. I don't have the spring spearhead. I don't have any of it.

He was going to kill me.

And I believed in him enough to let him do it.

Dres lifted his hand under my chin, guiding my focus back onto him and only him, audience be damned. I pushed away any nerves that were trying to find their way to the surface.

"Do you trust me?" he asked quietly, his deep voice rumbling the space between us.

He kept his hand under my chin. The inside of the tent was so quiet. People stopped chewing their popcorn, they stopped their cheers and chants, and even the mice that scurried the grounds were stopped.

Everyone's attention was stilled in this fragile moment. The intimacy could be shattered with the drop of a dime.

I straightened my spine, brushed my red curls away from my face, and nodded my head with assurance. "More than anything," I answered with the truth.

Dres' eyes softened with approval. It was the final nail in the coffin that I was more than happy to die in.

Leading back to the metal platform, I glanced at the structure that held my fate. It looked threatening, for sure, but it didn't scare me. With Dres, I felt safe. I felt unstoppable.

We met at the backside of the platform. With one arm under my knees and the other under my shoulder blades, he scooped me up honeymoon style. I wrapped my arm around his shoulder, spending these final moments admiring his tight muscles under my limb.

Then, I glanced up at his face, only to see him staring intensely into the crowd. I furrowed my eyebrows, confused. The guests have never been more than a passing thought in his mind during the acts. He has *never* cared about anyone in the audience.

I tried my best to follow what his eyes were looking at without moving my head completely. Whatever had his attention, I didn't want to bring more to it. From my peripherals, I couldn't see anything besides shadowed guests watching the show. His jaw flexed briefly before his grip on me tightened.

"Hey," I said, stealing his attention. His eyes quickly fell back onto mine, and a new look crossed his face—one that I'd never seen on him before.

I knew it was my turn to give him the reassurance he needed. I wanted to give him what he had constantly been giving me.

Illusion

Reaching up, I grazed my fingertips along the sharp edge of his jaw. His head turned to me completely, and a piece of dark hair fell over his eyes.

"You and me," I assured him in a whisper under the warm glow of the lights. "It's only us."

Even though I had all my faith and trust in him, it slightly unnerved me to see him slip away from me like this.

His face softened as he leaned into my touch. The warmth of his arms wrapped around me as his focus fell back to the illusion. Approaching the metal platform, he raised me up high and moved me away from his body, and I used some of my core strength to help him keep me balanced. He let me hover over the sharp, pointed pole, my back barely touching the tip.

In the standard illusion, I would be wearing everything needed to make this trick work. I would have a metal piece flush with my back that would fit over a fake, collapsing pole. The spear on the top would fall into the pole, allowing the top to flatten and fit into the piece in my back. I would lay on the metal board, and along with the muscles in my abdomen and legs, I would keep my body straight, creating the illusion that I was hovering using the magician's magic.

Then, with a press of a button, a tap of the shoe, the flick of the wrist, whatever, the machine in the pole would drop me, not delicately. At the same time, a small contraption on my stomach under my clothes would set off, making a new spearhead spring up and out of me.

My body would fall limp, and it would appear that I had been impaled with the spear and its pole.

Of course, I wasn't *really* impaled.

It was all in the timing.

But here, right now, with Dresden, I had nothing. No metal plate on my back, no spring on my stomach.

Only the hard, metal tip against the skin just an inch left of my spine, the shine in Dres' eyes, and trust.

"I'm going to ask you one last time, Willa," Dres' voice was firm and tight as he held me over the sharp, pointed metal. "Do you trust me?"

Everything led us to this moment.

The burn on my tongue.

The fist on Bram's face.

The mystery of the water that filled my lungs.

The arrow in my shoulder.

The night at his firepit.

The smoke exchange.

There wasn't a single fucking bone in my body that fought it.

"I trust you," I choked out, and those were the last words I could even think about saying before he dropped me.

An unexplainable sensation soared through every inch of my body. Every muscle tensed, every emotion flooded my senses, and I tried to inhale every bit of oxygen I could before I screamed.

I screamed so loud that I couldn't hear the faint sound of the crowd gasping in disbelief.

The muscles in my neck gave out as my head dropped backward. Gravity pulled my arms down toward the floor. Blood instantly pooled in my throat, and my screams turned into gargles.

Tipping my head up slowly, I looked to see the metal spear sticking out of my stomach, covered in blood and small chunks of my own inside matter. I screamed again and let my head drop back down. Gathering whatever leftover energy I had that wasn't wasted away in shock, I tried to reach for the steel pole that protruded from me but had no luck. My arms were left to dangle at my sides.

Tears streamed from the outside of my eyes, mirroring the streams of blood that dripped down the pole under me. My red, wavy hair draped down in a curtain below me, and I could feel it move with each minimal motion of my head.

The crowd was silent as they watched me slowly die.

As my blinks became slower, Dres leaned down to me. His hand found the back of my head and supported it firmly. I let myself rest in his hold as his face neared mine.

And one look at his expression told me all I needed to know.

There was not a single hint of worry, fear, remorse, or regret.

There was only adoration. In *me*.

My insides felt tangled around the pole as my body was scrambling to fix itself. More blood was rushing to the impact with a steady pulse to my stomach, but since the pole was still firmly lodged in me, there wasn't a heavy flow pouring out of me.

Yet.

Getting me off this structure and getting the pole *out* was a different story.

With his free hand, Dres gently touched my chin and directed my gaze to his—something he had done many times before.

My eyes were heavy, but I obeyed his guide. I looked at him with exhaustion, and he looked at me with protection. I could feel my body begin to tremble under the lights' glow.

Then, leaning even closer, I watched as he closed his own eyes. His lips parted, and if these were my final moments, leave it to Dres to finally give me what I wanted.

But he stopped only inches from me and gave me something else instead.

Thick, white smoke.

The same smoke from the hidden tent.

The feeling was cold as the vapor slipped into my mouth, snaked down my throat, and filled my lungs. My pores instantly opened, my thoughts cleared, my eyes closed, and my heart stopped. It was like oxygen times a hundred, nicotine times a thousand, and menthol times a million. It was pleasureful, it was passionate, it was revitalizing.

It was my revival.

My mind went blank as the smoke continued to enter me with ease. I didn't even have to inhale.

And that's when I noticed that I was no longer in pain.

In fact, I felt relaxed. I felt calm. I felt tranquil.

Oddly enough, the pole that protruded from my abdomen felt soothing. It was almost like it was massaging my core, caressing me in all the right places.

All the right places.

My thighs squeezed together at the sudden realization. This felt… good.

Dres' smoke began to taper off as he continued to hold the back of my skull. My legs began to shift at the pleasure he was feeding me, both through my mouth and his magic.

I could feel the palm of his free hand slide down the length of my body. His delicate touch was out of sight from the audience, although they could still see the movement of his arm.

But still, no one cared because they were either focused on the smoke shared between us or the bloody pole sticking out of my body.

His arm traced my legs and found the crook of my knees. He eagerly hooked himself under me. To my own surprise, I was able to keep myself level as the hand that cradled my head moved to the underside of my shoulders. It was the same position we were in only minutes ago.

With an effortless lift and pull, Dres hoisted me off the spear. An immense amount of pressure seeped through my torso, and I let out a cry of relief the moment I was free. The sound that came from the hollows of my throat wasn't the result of pain but rather a voice of satisfaction.

The volume of the crowd intensified as they watched blood pour out of the hole in my body. A few shrieks filtered through the air, along with shocked gasps and horrified cries.

The only people who didn't seem to be scared were Dres and me.

In fact, the entire time he was lifting me off the pole, he was gazing at me with a new shine in his eyes. I kept my stare on him, watching as his confidence poured out of him and into me.

I lifted my lips in a small smile, one that was only shared between us.

He gave the same smile right back.

Carrying me to the front of the stage, the entire audience seemed to hold their breath. Everyone stood up from their seats, waiting to see what was about to come of this.

"Deep breath for me," Dres whispered in my ear. With a heavy inhale, I closed my eyes and felt the hold of the oxygen in my lungs.

And with the expansion of the air, with the stretch of my chest, and with the opening of my ribs, I could feel the tightness again.

I blinked as my eyes instantly fell down to my torso. There was still a rip in my dress and fresh blood on the fabric, but the skin that covered my stomach was perfectly intact.

I looked back up at Dres, my eyes catching the dark freckle that I'd come to know so well. The smile that graced his lips doubled in size.

"Showtime, baby," Dres whispered in my ear once more, his breath sending a chill down the side of my neck.

Slowly lowering me to the floor, I planted my feet on the wooden stage. For a moment, I was nervous my legs would give out, leaving me as an unsteady body in front of everyone, but surprisingly, I had a good amount of strength in me. Whether it was from the adrenaline or from the smoke Dres gave me, it was keeping me up. And alert.

And astounded.

Dres' hand lingered on my waist for a moment, steadying me before sliding away. Hundreds of eyes were on me as I looked out to the crowd, unable to see anyone beyond the shadows of the spotlights. Dres lifted one of his arms, showcasing me in pride, as the crowd roared.

Clapping, cheering, whistling, everything. The tent went from a cold, dead silence to an incredible standing ovation.

I gave another small, modest smile before glancing down to my stomach again.

There was not a single scratch etched into my skin.

Even though I knew Dres had it in him, I was in just as much disbelief as the audience. I should know better by now. Dres is magical.

With the ease of a smirk still on his lips and the admiration full in his eyes, he shook his head in response as his gaze never left me. And just like every other night, he didn't look at the audience once.

He only looked at *me*.

Since it was our final show, I expected him to bow, wave, something.

But he didn't.

With the crowd still in a constant cheer, Dres approached me slowly. His focus on me went from proud and soft to heated and intense. His chin dipped as he looked down at me, the fervor in his expression only growing by the second.

The quickening pulse in my body expanded and pumped life into my needs. Having him in front of me—with a new set of accomplishments behind us and a whole new year ahead of us—gave me a new type of adrenaline.

A new type of want.

A new type of *trust*.

It was a hope on the horizon; it was a dream soon awakening.

I watched as his focus moved down to my lips, then back up to my eyes.

With hundreds of people around, there was no one here but us.

Before I could realize it, Dres' hands found the backs of my thighs. He swiftly lifted me up, my legs to his waist, my arms to his shoulders. My feet crossed at the ankles around his back as his hands supported me.

And he carried me off stage.

Our show was over, but our night was just beginning.

22

The door to my trailer burst open at my forceful shove. With my fist wrapped around Dres' white shirt, I pulled him inside and shut the door behind him. After a quick lock of the deadbolt, I turned and pressed my back to the door as Dres threw his black sweatshirt onto the couch.

The moment lingered in the stillness.

The moment.

Dres took one final step to me, closing the space that separated us. His dark hair fell in locked pieces over his forehead, creating shadowed lines over the heated expression he was giving me. He lifted his arms and pressed his palms onto the door behind me. His breathing began to speed up, his chest expanding and brushing against mine with every inhale.

I moved my hands to his sides, slowly easing them down before grabbing the hem of his shirt. I slid my palms onto his soft skin, my touch caressing his strong body.

It was the first time I had ever touched him intimately, and it was a line we were both waiting to finally cross.

With his hands still on the door, caging me in, he closed his eyes and pressed his forehead to mine.

"Willa," he muttered softly, his voice a deep grumble, almost as if he was saying my name to himself rather than to me.

To taste my name.

To keep me.

To *remember* me.

But then he moved his hand to the side of my face. His knuckles brushed against the curve of my jaw, his delicate embrace reaching and grasping the deepest parts of my soul.

Then, with his eyes still closed, his other hand followed suit. Both of his palms moved to the sides of my neck, his fingers woven into the roots of my hair, and his thumbs stroked the space right under my ears.

Who would've thought the gentlest of movements would make my knees instantly weak.

And with the slightest, subtlest inhale, Dres leaned in and pressed his lips to mine.

My eyes fluttered closed at the warmth of his mouth on mine. The tip of my nose brushed along the length of his as we moved our kiss as one. His tongue eased into my mouth and connected with mine. My heart couldn't stop skipping, my legs couldn't stop shaking, and my lungs couldn't stop holding the air I so desperately needed.

Dres gripped my neck as he pulled me into him. I continued to run my hands all over his body—from his chest to his stomach, from his shoulders to his waist. My fingertips grazed the trail of his spine, ran along the ridges of his ribs, and lined the indentations of his muscles.

Only pulling away for a second, Dres grabbed the back of his shirt, pulled it over his head, and tossed it aside.

The translation from my touch to the picture I had in my head didn't do it justice because Dres' body was incredible. My eyes studied every inch of him—from his rounded, strong shoulders, to his defined chest, and to his toned core. To me, he was the definition of perfect.

His lips were back on mine before I could memorize him more. And like his body, his kiss was just as divine.

Instead of wrapping his hands back on my neck, he moved them under my legs and lifted me once again. His motions were fluid and effortless as he carried me across the room. Since all single trailers had the same layout, he didn't even have to ask me where to go. He took me to the room along the back wall, kicked the door open, and laid me on the bed. Neither one of us bothered to turn on any lights.

Darkness coated the room as we existed in a new dynamic.

All we wanted was this, now, with no details or logistics.

With my back flat on the white comforter beneath me, my red hair splayed out in different directions, and Dres hovering above me, my heart began to swell.

Dres rested his forearms on either side of my head as he held himself up over me.

"Do you want this, Willa?" he asked in a whisper, breaking the comfortable silence.

Reaching up, I ran the tips of my fingers through his fallen hair. He wasn't asking me if I trusted him anymore. He was asking *me* to make the decision. He was asking if I wanted all of him.

He was asking if I trusted myself.

Do I trust myself?

The last time I fully gave myself to someone, it turned into something I hated. It mutated into something that could never evolve into love. It converted into a sickness, a disease, a poison for my soul.

But through that pain, I learned what wickedness looked like. I could easily spot what was not for me, what was not helping me grow, what was not playing in my favor. I was able to keep myself guarded while still enduring the theft of what was most valuable to me.

Myself.

The silence after his question must've been noticeable because Dres grabbed one of my hands and brought it up to his lips. He kissed each of my knuckles, leaving a trail of heat with every stamp of his affection.

And I knew, without a doubt, this was different.

I was pushed to my limits while still watching the safety net under me. I was at the brink of my sanity while standing with serenity. I was on the verge of fear while simultaneously wrapping myself in assurance.

I was taught the most important lesson in life.

Trust.

"Do you want this, Willa?"

My answer was the same exact answer I gave him less than an hour ago.

On the stage. Under the lights. In front of everyone.

"More than anything," I finally whispered. His loving gaze didn't change. Either he knew I was already in it, or my rejection wouldn't have changed anything between us.

Either way, it warmed me to know he was here for *me*, for *us*, and not for himself.

Lifting my back off the bed, I leaned up and kissed him. His lips molded into mine, fitting snugly in its heat. He grabbed the strap of my dress and pulled it down, then switched hands and did the same with the other side. I wiggled my body and shimmied the tight, ripped dress off, letting it fall to a heap onto the floor. Meanwhile, Dres unbuttoned his jeans, slipped his thumbs under the waistband of his boxer briefs, and slid everything down. His length bounded free, already raised and begging for attention. My eyes watched as he gripped the base and fisted himself, causing a bead of fluid to liquify at the head.

But in my gaze, my eyes caught sight of black numbers written horizontally across the middle of his left thigh.

1442151132

My head tilted at the tattoo, and the sudden memory of the night at the tattoo tent came back to me—the way he tensed when I asked if he had any ink, the way the answer was never addressed, and the way the topic was dismissed.

Now, I have my answer.

Dres didn't have to follow my line of sight to figure out what I was looking at. He brought his knee up and pressed it onto the bed, allowing me to get a better look. The numbers were still bold and crisp, even if the saturation had faded a bit.

"They knocked me out one day when I was fifteen. I woke up with a stinging pain in my thigh only to look down and see this."

He motioned to his leg carelessly.

As if he knew what I was going to ask, he answered for me anyway. "I don't know what it means. Some identification number, probably. Some stupid fucking way to diminish me more than I already was."

My eyes left the tattoo and moved back up to his face.

"I tried everything to get it off and out of my skin. I tried scrubbing it away in the shower until my skin was raw. I tried to fucking cut it out of me. I tried all of my abilities. Whatever they put in me was more than ink because it can't be removed. Or covered."

I lifted my hand and grazed my touch along the numbers. There were faded scars around the black numbers, small white lines from past attempts to free himself from the memories.

Dres' story was unlike anything I'd ever heard before, and the truth of it broke something inside of me.

I've always heard of these things happening, but I've never met someone it actually happened to. It made everything more… real.

"Don't," Dres whispered with a gravelly tone.

I looked up at him again, and it was like he already knew what I was thinking.

What I was *feeling*.

"Don't let *that*," he said, referring to the piece of his backstory he just gave me, "take away from *this*," he added, slowly returning to me. I leaned back down onto the bed as he crawled over my body, both of us bare and ready.

"I'd go through all of that again if it would bring me back to you."

His words ran through me like ice, freezing me with their shock. He was blunt. He was serious.

And yet, something felt off.

His voice was deep, but it was desperate.

His body was needy, but his guard felt up.

His desires were obvious, but his emotions were untraceable.

"There's a magic about you, Willa, one that is impossible to replicate. Everyone in the world can try to bottle up what you have, but no one will ever be able to capture the glow you radiate."

His lips found mine again in a quick yet passionate embrace.

"Not even me."

My heart thumped against my chest. It was the nicest thing anyone had ever said to me.

Ever.

Dres' hands skimmed every inch of me as his gaze absorbed me. The softness of my stomach met the hardness of his calloused palms. The curves of my hips met the straightened bone of his jaw as his kisses trailed down my body. The warm breath that slid past his lips met the chilled skin covered in goosebumps.

My muscles tensed under him as his lips trailed down to my center, intensifying the slickness that was already there.

With each kiss, his tongue dipped out, caressing me in affection. His mouth lingered over my most sensitive area, and all I wanted was for him to dive in.

And with the most tender and easy motions, that's exactly what he did.

His tongue stroked my pussy with one slow, fluid act, and my whole body instantly succumbed to him. My legs weakened, my chest heaved, and my throat let out a low, pent-up moan.

He repeated the action, over and over, until my back arched off the bed and my hands gripped his smooth hair. My fingertips dug into his scalp as I pulled him into me harder, letting my wild inhibitions take over.

The enjoyment was written all over his face as his eyes went from closed and relaxed to open, lustful, and locked on me.

And through his licks and kisses, a smile spread across his lips.

His head felt so fucking good between my legs.

And he didn't even need magic to do it.

"Dresden."

My voice ached in echoes of the room. He lifted his chin to look at me, a hint of a glimmer in his eyes. The same ache that was in my voice, the same need that I tried to convey to him, was there in his gaze.

We both needed this.

With my body already close to the edge, I watched as Dres lifted himself up and positioned himself on top of me. He angled his body so he was leaning off to one side but still hovering over me.

My eyes fell down to his lips, where my own liquids coated his skin, and I lifted a finger to trace his full bottom lip.

He grabbed that same hand and kissed it. My heart fluttered at the gesture.

And with a simple, flawless motion, he slipped himself inside me. My lips parted at his fullness and the way he fit so comfortably.

The moment his hips met mine was the moment he dropped his head down to my chest in surrender.

"Fuck," he whispered, and I could feel the pulse of his cock throb inside of me.

He pulled back and thrust again, and it felt just as good as the first time.

My hands grabbed his arms, and the tips of my fingers dug into his biceps. I could feel the chill run through him and the goosebumps arise under my palms.

The feeling of us, as one, was something completely extraordinary and otherwise unexplainable.

This was like nothing I had ever felt before. Nothing compared to the emotions that ran through my body at his embrace.

Illusion

Everything I thought I knew about sex went out the window the moment his body fell into mine.

Dres' breath coated my skin as he panted through his thrusts, and as my clit brushed against him, my arousal soared to new heights.

As I wrapped my legs around his waist, I spread my knees open as wide as they could go, allowing Dres to fully push everything inside. His lips found and kissed the side of my neck, my jawbone, my cheek, then my lips.

And, for the first time, I found someone whose kiss felt like home.

"I am tied to you," Dres spoke against my lips and between thrusts. "And every cell, every breath, every thought you have is tied to me. You and I are always as one."

I looked to Dres, who was already staring at me. His gaze never faltered, his thrusts never stuttered, and his confidence never failed.

I've never been in love. There was a point where I thought I had something that could go somewhere, but it never did.

But now, in this moment, I knew it was the closest I had ever been to the feeling.

Dres gave a final shake of his head as his length hit the one spot it was looking for.

"It's you, Willa. *It's you.*"

My soul felt weightless as his words paralleled my thoughts. Dres let out a deep groan, one that prompted the wave of pleasure I wanted to reach. My eyes fluttered closed as his own undoing triggered mine. Between the emotions behind his words and the feeling of his skin on mine, I unraveled underneath him.

The orgasm stretched me in hundreds of different directions, sending me up and down, front to back, to this world and the next. And as I felt Dres pour himself inside of me, with his trembling arms holding himself up above, I couldn't find my balance.

I didn't *want* to find my balance.

I wanted him to catch me, to hold me, to create my new equilibrium.

I wanted us as one, always.

The only sound in the quiet room was our attempt to catch our breath. With Dres still inside of me, he rested against my side with his weight on the bed. I grabbed a blanket from the foot of the mattress, pulled it up, and covered us both.

There was nothing else to be said.

We experienced it all.

We felt everything.

And what we couldn't say with our voices, we could easily say with our eyes.

But as time carried on, with our bodies sated from the night and exhausted from the week of adrenaline, my eyes began to blink slower, and my lids grew heavy.

Dres slowly raised his hand to brush a lock of hair away from my face. It was gentle, it was meaningful, and in that moment, it was perfect.

He was perfect.

We were perfect.

1442151132

Fuck.

I can't fucking do this.

With her vibrant red hair and her soft, tanned skin…

Fuck.

I stood up from the bed, careful not to cause her to stir, and I pulled all my clothes back on. Her eyes were gently closed, her breathing was even, and her body was as relaxed as I'd ever seen. All I wanted to do was crawl back under those covers, feel her warmth, and fall asleep next to her.

But I couldn't.

Every bone in my body was screaming at me to stay with her.

But I *couldn't*.

There was too much of a risk.

There was too much on the line.

There was too much to lose, and I would *never* forgive myself if I lost her.

Illusion

I don't know if it was her steady persistence, her strength, or her growth over the last week that led us to this moment. Maybe it was all of it.

All I knew was I wouldn't take back any of it.

After pulling on my sweatshirt, I stood over the bed for a prolonged moment. Despite all the things she's been through in her life, she still looked peaceful while sleeping. I envied her because I hardly ever get good sleep anymore.

But I know that if I were to fall asleep next to her, I would get the best sleep of my life.

She just radiates that comfort.

Fuck.

Slowly reaching down, I brushed some of the hair away from her face. Her lids were still covered in silver glitter, her cheeks were a warm, flushed pink, and her lips were full and plump.

The lips that I couldn't get enough of.

Her kisses were an instant fuel. One kiss from her could keep me going for a lifetime.

And for now, the memory of her lips is all I'll have to push on.

The blankets came up to her chest, covering her as she laid on her side. My eyes trailed down her neck, rounded her shoulders, and coasted over her smooth arms. Black ink poked out from the edge of the comforter, and I leaned over to take a last look at the healed tattoo I placed on her ribs.

It was a night I would never forget.

I slipped on my shoes and headed out the door, leaving it unlocked for the time being.

The night was still alive, as it had been every other night this week.

Even from the back lots, I could still feel the pulse of life from the main grounds. Music was blasting from the tents. Lights were flashing. People were laughing.

Although only six hours were left of the week, the events weren't even close to dying down.

Which meant I only had six hours left to do what I needed to do.

I pulled my black hood up over my head and began going from trailer to trailer. I grazed my hand along each front step, each door frame, and every doorknob. I let my fingertips release my abilities onto the solid objects, so whenever anyone touched one of these things, it would work in my favor.

I've done it before. I'm sure I'll do it again.

No one will remember me once they touch what I've touched.

I made my rounds through all the trailers until they all had what they needed, and then I walked along the path, touching the wooden fence as well.

Anyone who takes the shortcut will no longer remember me.

As I filtered my way through the crowded grounds, I tried to touch everything I could. I touched Vark's office door. I touched every tent entrance. Every carnival game. Every food stand. Even if it was a quick brush of my fingertips, that's all that was needed. Any contact will erase everything about me in a person's mind.

"Hey, Dres!" a voice shouted at me, and I turned to look. It was the man that made the roasted almonds. Troy, I think Willa called him.

I gave him a polite smile and headed into the tent.

"I heard you guys were incredible. I'm disappointed I didn't get to see it, but everyone is saying how good it was."

I gave him a simple nod. "Thank you."

He rested his arms over the glass counter, leaned in, and motioned for me to do the same.

With heaviness in my chest, I leaned forward to hear his words.

Illusion

"Treat her good, okay?" he hushed. "She deserves it."

Fuck.

Fucking damn it.

I glanced at him and gave him another nod. His appreciative expression never faded as he reached for a bag of almonds and tossed them to me. "On the house."

I quickly looked down at the bag, then back up to Troy. I pushed down any fucking remorseful feelings I had.

Because now was not the time.

Extending my hand, I reached over the counter. Troy took it in a grateful handshake, and I watched as the friendly recognition faded before my eyes.

Some people deserve the invasive process of my mental manipulation.

Most people don't.

But no matter what, the feeling I get while watching someone forget never subsides.

Troy's eyes narrowed, and his eyebrows furrowed. Hesitation lingered on his tongue for a moment before he spoke.

"Can I help you with something?" he asked in his best customer service voice, as if we hadn't already had a conversation.

I held up the small bag of almonds. "Thank you. Have a good night."

Troy nodded, still confused, then turned back to his work. I walked out of the tent, brushing my fingertips along the tent's entrance for anyone else who decided to come in before the morning appeared.

Multiple guests approached me, praising the show they had seen. I made it a point to shake all their hands and then watched as the glistening light fell from their eyes.

They loved the show, but suddenly, they couldn't remember why.

Now, I know there will be people that slip between the cracks. I can't touch everyone or everything, but I can get through to most.

And the people that do remember me will never know my name. All they will have is the memory of the show and friends who don't remember what they're talking about.

Word of me will not make it far, and hopefully, it will not find the one person I didn't want it to find.

The person that set all this in motion.

The man I saw in the audience only hours ago, Dr. Lacuna.

He was watching me from the crowd, watching as I performed the magic he knew so well.

The magic *he* created.

The magic *he* injected into my mother while she was pregnant with me.

It was the first time I had seen him since the day I escaped from the University. His memory was never erased, even though I tried to wipe myself from him.

It didn't work.

It didn't work on *any* of them.

So, when he looked at me and I found him in the crowd, I tried to keep myself neutral. Even though Willa saw me and noticed a new hesitation, I still tried to remain expressionless. I didn't want Dr. Lacuna to know I saw him. I needed to act as if everything was normal and carry on as normal, even though, in that instant, I knew it was the end.

The end of my time here on the island.

The end of my time at the carnival.

The end of me and Willa.

I couldn't bring her into this mess. I couldn't chance being with her when it would only put her in danger. They would easily use her against me and use her to get to me. I couldn't risk losing her when I finally just got her.

Even going back to her trailer and taking all of her was putting her on the line. But I couldn't leave without knowing what she tasted like, even if it was only for one night.

Illusion

I needed to know how she felt under my skin, under my touch, under my tongue.

I'd do it all again.

But now, I have to leave. I can't stay knowing they know I'm here. I don't want to become an experiment again.

And I definitely don't want to put Willa through the trials I knew I would face.

She loves this island too much.

Her friends are here; her life is here.

I would never take that from her.

After finishing my way around the entire island and touching everything I could, I made my way back to the trailers. The sun was beginning to rise, and the grounds were quieter at the signal of the week's close. Most people had already gone to bed or back to their trailers to get ready to leave. Tents were starting to close down, lights were turning off, and performers were finally getting their chance to rest.

I found myself back at Willa's trailer.

I stepped inside, only to find her still sleeping in the same exact spot I left her. She was asleep on her stomach, with her bare back exposed and her arm crooked over her head.

Careful not to make any noise, I squatted down to be face-level with her. Her sleep was so deep, and she looked so content. It made me happy to know I had something to do with it.

My eyes filled with a new emotion, one that I hadn't felt in so long that I almost didn't recognize it.

Sorrow.

I quietly cleared my throat as I watched her breathe.

"I'm coming back for you, Willa. I don't know if it will be in a month, or a year, or five years. But please, if you remember anything, remember that. I will find my way back to you. I promise."

My words choked in my throat, threatening to break me as I spoke.

I brushed my fingertips along her forehead, then down to her neck, pushing away her hair gently.

"I'm so sorry, Willa. Please forgive me."

More than anything, I wanted to grab her hands and kiss them. I wanted to lean close and breathe her in. I wanted to take her in my arms and stay there.

But I couldn't chance waking her. I didn't want to make this harder than it already was.

So, with one final swipe of my fingers, I skimmed them along her forehead, erasing all of me from her conscious memory. But one thing I'll always have is her dreams. I'll always be there until I can fully be with her again.

24

Sunlight spilled into the room, casting illuminated beams along my comforter. I blinked, squinting my eyes at the sudden brightness.

It took me a second to figure out that I was sleeping… in my own bed… naked.

Why was I naked?

How did I get here?

Damn, I must've been really tired last night.

Pushing the blankets away and swinging my legs over the side, I climbed out of bed. I glanced to my dress on the floor and tilted my head curiously.

Was that a hole?

Was it ripped?

And why was there blood on it?

I glanced down at my own body. There was no blood on me. Not a scratch, not a cut, nothing.

I brushed the thought away with a hum of confusion. *Did I drink last night?* Maybe I can ask Six. Usually, if I drink too much, he's the first one to fill me in on everything.

Then again, I wasn't even sure where I put my phone.

After a quick scan of the room, I found it lying on my dresser. I grabbed it and tapped the screen.

12:48 PM.

No new messages.

Holy Hell, it was after noon already?

How long was I asleep?

I looked back at my phone, checked the date, and paused.

Wait a minute.

The Carnival week was over.

The guests had to be gone and off the island by now. The main plane usually leaves around twelve every year on the final day. And somehow, I slept through the departure.

I dropped my hand to my side and glanced around the room. I needed to figure everything out. I must've been drinking last night since my head was in such a mindless fog, but even after drinking, smoking, or both, I'd never completely blacked out before.

My eyes drifted to the full-length mirror in the corner of the room, and I caught sight of my reflection. I was still naked, but it was a little black drawing that drew me in. I walked over to the mirror, turned to my side, and stared at it.

A small tattoo of a single stem of flowers.

The corner of my lips curled up, and I couldn't help the foreign bliss the drawing gave me, even through the confusion that presented itself.

I ran my hand over the inked skin. It was smooth, the lines were delicate but bold, and the black ink was fresh and contrasted beautifully against my skin.

My mind reeled back to the tattoo tent, with me laying on the table, my eyes closed as the stinging sensation scratched against my back.

But in that memory, that's all I could remember.

Why this flower? Who drew it on me?

And why don't I remember it healing?

I had no recollection of it itching, of a shirt rubbing against it and reminding me it was there, or anything.

It was just… here.

God, I desperately needed to talk to Six.

I grabbed my phone, sent him a text, then proceeded to get dressed. I pulled on a pair of jeans, a grey hoodie, and wrapped my messy hair back into a ponytail before brushing my teeth.

I crossed the living room and headed to the front door towards my shoes.

And that's when I saw it.

On my kitchen island, sitting right in the middle, was a glass bowl. It was filled with water, a few green plants, and a little stone house. A black and white fish swam slowly across the front of the glass, its fins flowing in the waves of the water.

On the front of the glass was a single yellow post-it note.

Jane

Jane? Did I win a fish last night and name it Jane?

Staring at the paper, I studied the name with yet another wave of confusion.

The name wasn't written in my handwriting.

I left the paper on the counter, letting the adhesive on the back stick to the granite surface.

I slipped on my shoes, locked the front door behind me, and headed to the main grounds. With all of the guests gone and the week over, the island was eerily quiet. The place almost seemed deserted in the wake of the events.

I hopped over the wooden fence and made my way to one of the main paths. A few workers were tearing down their tents and disassembling their structures until next year.

"Willa!" A voice called out behind me, and I turned to look.

It was Six, thank God. He looked well-rested and happy. He jogged up to me, wearing a sweatsuit that was the polar opposite of his performance attire.

"How are you doing, babe?" he asked as he wrapped his arm around my shoulder. We found a nearby picnic table that had yet to be removed and sat on it.

"I'm good," I hesitated, even though it wasn't a lie. I felt amazing physically; it was my mind that was in a blur. "Can I ask you something?"

He nodded as he pulled out a carton of cigarettes. "Go for it. Want one?" he asked, holding the box out to me.

I shook my head. "No, thanks."

Six didn't seem surprised by my answer, and I didn't feel sad turning it down. I remember trying to ease up on smoking for the week, but I couldn't recall the reason why.

"Were we together last night?" I asked, getting straight to the point.

"No. I was performing. You went straight home after your show."

"My show," I confirmed. "Did you watch it?"

Six exhaled the drag of his cigarette. "No, I just told you I was performing. I heard it was good, though."

"You did?" I asked, hoping to get a bit more information. "From who?"

He shrugged. "Just around. I didn't really hear any specifics." A pause shifted between us as he took another pull of his smoke. "Why? Is everything okay?"

"Yeah," I said, my voice unconvincing. "I'm fine. Really. I just… I'm having trouble remembering last night."

Six looked at me with wandering eyes, his focus intense on my face.

"I can't remember most of the week, actually. Bits and pieces are still there. And I can't recall the explanation for the things I *do* remember."

"Like what?"

"Well, for starters, there's a fish in my house."

"You won a fish?" Six laughed.

"I think so. Her name is Jane."

"Jane? Willa, *babe*. Of anything in the world you could name a fish, you pick Jane?"

"Shut up," I dismissed. "And there's this…"

I pulled up the side of my sweatshirt, exposing the small tattoo along the side of my back.

Six's eyes widened. "Holy shit! You got ink? That's badass."

I lifted a small smile. "I did. I love it, actually. But I don't remember why I got it."

Six let out another chuckle before dropping the butt of his cigarette and extinguishing it with his shoe. "Sounds like you had a fun night. Did you go to *Onyx?*"

I furrowed my brows, trying to collect any memory I could find. "Not that I remember."

"Maybe a guest gave you a bump of something. Maybe it was way stronger than you expected."

Propping up my elbow, I rested my cheek against my fist. I didn't want to say no to Six because his explanation was a definite possibility.

But I've had hangovers before, and I've done a few drugs here and there. I've woken up with a pounding headache, and I've even woken up in a daze.

But every single time, I'd gained my bearings. I've been able to remember the night before, even if the memories took a few minutes to appear.

I'd always been able to keep my control.

What made last night—last *week*—so different?

"Willa?" A voice snapped me out of my thoughts. I looked over at Six, but it wasn't him who said my name.

It was Bram.

"Willa, please. We need to talk."

25

"Please."

His tone was desperate as he stood in front of the picnic table with a cut lip and a giant black eye. His clothes were unusually scuffed and dirty, his hair was slightly tangled, and his shoes were a gross shade of brown. He glanced to Six—who didn't seem to give a single fuck he was here—then moved his eyes back to me. I looked down at the arm he held by his side and noticed the white cast covering his wrist.

"God, Bram, are you okay?"

"I'm fine."

"What did you do?"

"I tripped over some string lights," he said, lifting his arm to inspect the hardened plaster. "Landed wrong."

"Heard you got into it with one of Troy's guys," Six piped up from my side as he lit a new cigarette.

"You did?" I asked Bram. "When?"

"Uh, the night before last," Bram answered, his good hand lifting and brushing the back of his head.

There was something deep in me that wasn't feeling any of this. I didn't believe Bram, I didn't agree with Six, and I didn't understand my own state of mind. Something was going on, and I needed to figure it out.

"Vark let you perform like that?" My question was coated in disbelief.

"I managed," he confirmed. "*We* managed."

Getting up and stepping off the picnic table, I approached Bram. I felt nothing as I stood and stared at him. I didn't feel fear, I didn't feel apprehension, I didn't feel disgust. There was no regret, no sympathy, no dread.

I felt *nothing*.

He had nothing over me anymore. There wasn't a single part of me that couldn't push back against Bram and anything he would try to pull.

And that was a new feeling.

One that I enjoyed.

"So, we kicked ass, huh?" I asked Bram, who looked almost as confused as I felt.

I knew that look. He was hiding something.

When he didn't answer, I tried a different angle.

"Did Vark punish you for that?" I motioned to his hand. "You know there's no fighting allowed."

"Yeah," he started, his expression uneasy. "I had to help out around the grounds last night. That's why my shoes are covered in shit."

On instinct, I crinkled my nose. After he mentioned it, it did look like he worked really hard last night. His appearance proved it.

"Did you do anything fun afterward?" I inquired curiously.

Bram shook his head. "Hell no. I went home and crashed. I was fucking wrecked."

So, Bram wasn't the reason why I woke up naked. Thank fucking God.

I already had an inkling that he wasn't the reason anyway, but I'm thankful to have it confirmed. And judging by the odd look of fear in his eyes—fear of *me*—he didn't seem like he wanted to do anything more than have a simple conversation with me.

What in the actual fuck was happening?

"Ah, good to see everyone's here," a phlegmy voice spoke to the right, and the three of us turned to look.

"Hey, Boss," Six nodded to Vark, who walked up to us with his hands in his pockets. His signature cigar was nowhere to be seen, and he looked happy, even pleased with all of us and the success of the week. His hair was still slicked over in a thin combover, his button-down shirt stretched as his stomach protruded over the waistband of his pants, and his suspenders hung down at his sides.

He approached Bram and jostled his shoulders as he gave a playful smile. "You learn your lesson yet?"

Bram nodded, not returning the forced cheer. "Yes, sir."

"Good," Vark replied, then turned to Six and me. "Where's Dres?"

I furrowed my eyebrows as Six and I both answered, "Who?"

Vark straightened his spine and dropped his arm from Bram. "Dresden?" he asked quietly, unsure of himself.

I looked to Bram and Six, who also didn't seem to know who Vark was referring to.

"What the fuck kind of name is *Dresden?*" Bram sneered, and it was the last thing I heard before my mind tuned everything out. Their voices became background noise as I ran my hand over my mouth.

Dres. Dresden.

Why did that name sound so familiar?

"Dres," I rolled the name on my tongue in a whisper.

I did it again.

"Dres."

And again.

With each mention of his name, a flash of a memory flickered through my vision.

Illusion

First, it was a flame.

Second, it was water.

Next, it was my tattoo.

Lastly, it was the image of someone's skin on mine.

But no matter how many times I said the name, I couldn't figure out where I knew it from. I couldn't figure out how these pictures were appearing. The sound rang true in my ears, and the name felt too familiar on my tongue to dismiss it.

But with everyone puzzled and their eyes on me, I had no choice but to leave the name in the fleeting vapor of confusion.

Dres.

I didn't know a Dres.

26

Vast, open waters lapped against my ankles as I stood in the point's coast. Indigo-colored waves crested with white foam ran upon the shore in a steady pattern, matching the consistent pace of my breathing.

Nighttime was approaching, but I had no desire to leave.

Calmness washed over me, easing me into a state of relief as a new presence found me. Echoed thoughts were silenced the second I felt him with me.

"Nightfall is my favorite time," I whispered, hoping he could hear me over the sounds of the crashing waves.

The footsteps at my back stopped, and I waited patiently for the next moments. A brisk wind brushed along the side of my face and neck, whipping my hair to the side, and with a hand, I gently gathered it all to one shoulder.

Right as I was about to close my eyes, slip away, and find the reach of my realities, a hand rested on the curve of my left side, right along my ribcage.

Keeping me here, in this world, was the touch of that hand.

One step was all it took for me to turn around, to face my desire, to see exactly who I'd been waiting for.

Never would I ever stop chasing the reality of this realm.

An intense stare, a sharp jawline, and a sorrowful expression met me in my welcoming confrontation.

I lost all the breath in my lungs at the sight of him, even though the steady waves continued to breathe behind me.

Staring at me with a gaze so deprived, he remained melancholy as I asked one simple question.

"Tonight, you'll come back for me?"

His blue eyes searched mine as he remained silent, and the stillness in his absent answer was achingly unbearable.

Every moment that passed felt like a slow and steady death, easing me into a place where I'll never find him again.

Brightness from the sunset faded, allowing the twilight to dwindle down to nothing. As night consumed us, the picture of him slowly disappeared into the darkening shadows around us.

Drinking him in, I forced my memory to keep his image, just in case tonight would be the last time I would ever see him.

Grounds under my feet felt unsteady, the winds beside me felt fleeting, and the flames in my soul felt like they were beginning to dim.

Unbinding myself from this state of delirium is something I couldn't do, no matter how much sense it would make to do so.

"*Yes*" was the word that lingered, that begged to be spoken but never came, even as I woke and transferred myself into the conscious world.

27

Two Years Later

The blade sunk into the side of the box, sliding easily in the small wooden slit. I angled the metal perfectly, careful not to place it in a spot where it didn't belong.

The crowd gasped when they saw the shiny sword come out of the other side of the box. I smiled at the sound.

The final dagger slid in from above, the handle thumping against the top frame as the length reached its limit.

With all swords buried to the hilt in the box, the illusion was complete. There was no way anyone could fit in the box with the insane amount of metal tangled inside.

At least, that's what the audience was supposed to think.

One by one, the blades disappeared from the box, and they slid out without a single drop of blood on them.

A part of me was saddened at the lack of crimson. The illusion would have been more exciting and believable if some sort of injury was involved.

Grabbing the last handle, I pulled the sword out from the right side of the box. It was the final blade and the last bit of the performance.

Illusion

I grabbed the door of the box and swung it open, revealing a happy and unharmed Bram.

He stepped out, shirtless, chiseled, and oiled, and it took all my willpower not to drop my fake smile and roll my eyes. His shoulder-length dark hair fanned as he stepped out in *only* a pair of jeans, with his chest glistening and his arms open wide. The women in the crowd went wild at his appearance.

But then Bram looked over at me, lifted one arm, and showed gratitude to me.

The rest of the audience joined in cheering for our flawless performance.

Our *fake*, flawless performance.

Everything Bram and I did was perfect. Every trick we performed went without a hitch.

But the emptiness in the acts never subsided because that's all it was.

An *act*.

An *illusion*.

None of this was real. The magic was fabricated. The chemistry between Bram and I was nonexistent. The adrenaline I used to experience never showed itself anymore.

I still loved performing. I still loved the island, the carnival, and the magic.

But there was something missing.

A piece, a part, a detail.

I could never figure out what it was.

It's been exactly two years since I've felt this way. Two years with the inability to fix my mind. Two years of skating by, not knowing when this feeling would ease up or if it would ever go away.

I thought the feeling would finally subside a year after it began, when the next week of the carnival approached. Bram led our shows as the magician, and between my confusion and his indifference, it simply wasn't working. The dynamic between us had shifted. We were both unhappy in our roles, with him as the overseer and me leading the hidden secrets of our tricks.

So, halfway through the week, we switched.

I became the magician, and he became the assistant.

Shockingly, it was easy. He knew all the back doors to the illusion, and I knew how to stand there and look pretty, so it worked.

Plus, when the women saw him unscathed, it gave him a new high that felt similar to the ones he used to experience. He thrived off the glorious attention.

So, if attention's what he wants, attention's what he gets.

To my surprise, Bram has been good to me these past two years. He hasn't tried to cross any lines, he hasn't looked at me with need in his eyes, and he even stopped calling me by that stupid nickname.

I don't know what changed, but I was appreciative.

We worked well together, and that was it. We practiced, we performed, then we went our separate ways.

Our role reversal worked for a bit. I felt better, lighter, and more at ease with stepping out onto the stage every night. The difference worked in our favor.

But after the show ended, the lights dimmed, and I crawled into bed, the dreams didn't stop.

They *never* stopped.

For seven hundred and thirty days, I've dreamt about the same person.

The same man.

Every. Single. Night.

He came to me, with his strong arms and outstretched hand, and wrapped me in his warm body. With his dark hair and his blue eyes, he found me.

But I had no idea who he was.

And every morning, when I would open my eyes and glance around the sunlit room, a new crack would form in my heart at the acknowledgement that it was only a dream.

I couldn't physically touch him.

Illusion

I couldn't feel him, see him, meet him.

I only saw him when I couldn't be with him.

I didn't even know if he was a real person. Maybe he was just a figment of my imagination, or pieces of different people I've met jumbled together.

And that's the truth that hurt the most. That's all he'll ever be.

An illusion.

I've found myself aching to sleep. I've tried to force myself to sleep for days to find him. I've tried chasing him into consciousness; I've tried following him from realm to realm.

But every time I wake up, I wake up empty.

I wake up alone.

I wake up with the fear that my dreams will stop.

I wake up knowing it could be the last time I'll ever see him.

But the comfort I feel when I sleep—when I dream of him and feel him with me—destroys the agony I feel the second I wake up.

I would sleep forever if that meant I could be with him.

Bram led me to the front of the stage, where we both proceeded to take our bows. Bram did it first, and everyone cheered. He deserved it, after all, because he was the main reason why the tricks did as well as they did.

The assistant is always the one who holds the *trust* in the magic.

Bram then turned to me and began clapping. The crowd cheered for me, and I began to take a small bow.

But before I could bend at the waist, my eyes locked on someone in the audience. He was standing toward the back of the tent, with his face in the shadows and his blue eyes piercing through mine.

Blue eyes I'd seen hundreds of times. There was no mistaking those eyes.

My heart fell into the pit of my stomach as I looked at the man from my dreams.

Standing here, in the same tent as me.

I swallowed the shock as my body instantly grew weak.

Was I dreaming? Was this real?

How did I know if this was real?

The audience continued cheering for Bram and me, but the sounds didn't register. It was as if the world suddenly turned mute, and nothing else mattered except the person across the tent.

I knew it was now or never.

Without hesitation, I jumped off the stage, stumbling in my landing before catching my footing.

With the shine of the spotlight out of my eyes, I could see his face more clearly.

Bruises circled both eyes, shielding the unmistakable dark freckle under the center of his right eye.

Dried blood covered his split lip.

Discoloration seeped into his skin.

But more than that, he looked somber.

He looked *hurt*, both physically and emotionally.

It was an expression that never appeared in my dreams. Every time I saw him, he was smiling, he was healthy, he was happy.

This wasn't how I remembered him.

I pushed my way through the crowd, squeezing past the clapping guests. Their praises to me fell on deaf ears. I refused to blink, just in case the man was, in fact, a dream. I didn't want to lose him.

Not now.

I fought through the pats on the back and the eagerness of those who wanted to talk to me, all while my eyes were on the man from the home of my delirium.

As I was nearing him, with my legs gaining speed desperately and my chest struggling to breathe, he turned to his right to head towards the tent's exit.

No.

No, no, *no.*

As he turned, I saw a flash of a tattoo on the left side of his neck. It was a vertical drawing, one that I recognized immediately.

It was the same exact drawing I had on my side. The same flowers I looked at every single day.

Illusion

I struggled to weave my way through the guests as I watched the man slip out of the tent.

I wanted to call out to him, to scream for him to keep his attention, but the linger of his unknown name escaped my tongue.

"Wait, please," I shouted over the sea of people, my words hitting his back as he left.

Through the partial opening of the tent, I watched him move farther and farther away.

There was one last thing I wanted to say. One last chance to grab his attention.

"Let me go or take me with you."

I begged for him. I cried for him. I ached for him.

I wanted, more than anything, to go with him.

But if he wasn't going to have me, I wanted him to release me.

As much as I needed him in my dreams and longed to see him every night, the pain of waking without answers was something I wasn't sure I could endure much longer.

I pushed to the edge of the crowd and broke free. The fresh, nighttime air welcomed me as I stumbled out of the tent, my eyes immediately scanning the grounds for him.

But under the clear stars and cloudless skies, he was gone.

More guests lingered on the paths, existing in their own worlds, oblivious to the one thing I just lost.

Tears spilled out from both eyes as I planted my palm on my chest, unable to steady my racing heart and anxious breathing.

The broken fractures from waking without him set the blueprint for the shatter of my whole heart.

My entire world felt destroyed.

He was gone.

And now, all I could do was go to sleep.

There was a hidden ache in my throat and an onset of tears waiting to be unlocked as I swung open the door to my trailer. I wanted to wait until I got back to my home to let my emotions flow.

I didn't need anyone seeing me like this. I didn't want to explain why I couldn't help but feel connected to someone from my dreams.

Someone that turned out to be a real person.

Someone who felt the same way based on the matching hurt expression on his face.

So, why did he leave?

I shut the door behind me and pressed my back to it. I blinked up at the ceiling as I tipped my head, wanting to keep the tears inside just a little bit longer.

My chest was heavy. My eyes were tired.

My mind was running.

After a minute against the door, I pushed myself up and headed to the bedroom.

I'll shower tomorrow. At this point, I'll even sleep in my show makeup. I'm too mentally exhausted to care about anything except sleeping.

And dreaming.

As I approached the kitchen island, I tossed my sweatshirt on the counter and reached for Jane's fish food. She swam franticly across the glass, knowing it was time for her to eat.

But when I picked up the small plastic bottle, a yellow Post-it note stuck to the granite surface grabbed my attention.

And in that moment, I knew this wasn't over.

This wasn't even close to being over.

Because on that Post-it note was a drawing.

A drawing that changed everything.

A forget-me-not.

A small glimmer of hope sprang to life deep in the valleys of my heart.

He was here.

He knew me, he knew my tattoo, he knew my dreams.

Illusion

As I picked up the Post-it note while searing the drawing into my memory, I felt a warm presence at my back.

It was a feeling I had dreamt about but also recognized in the flesh. It was all too familiar.

It was all too *real*.

Large, warm hands found my waist, and I welcomed the touch immediately. My eyes fell closed at the heat, and I didn't need to turn around to know who it was.

His head bent down to my neck, and I tilted my head to allow him in. His breath was warm against my cold skin, and his lips grazed along the curve of my ear.

"Do you trust me?"

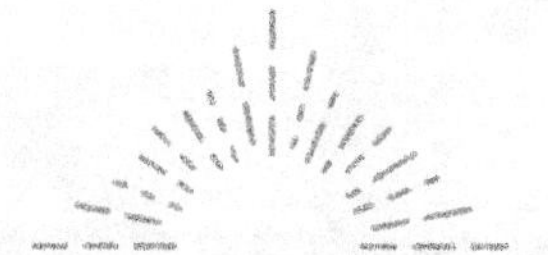